COMETS

COMETS

By

Joseph Allen Costa

For Dad

TABLE OF CONTENTS

Sundays too my father got up early
and put his clothes on in the blueblack cold,
then with cracked hands that ached
from labor in the weekday weather made
banked fires blaze. No one ever thanked him.

From *Those Winter Sundays* by Robert Hayden

Sinners and Saints

Juan and I had just finished putting the last of the screws into a base unit for a kitchen and we set it upright, when I looked up to see a sinewy black man standing in front of the shop. At first glance, I thought it was Sarge, waiting to speak to my dad, but Sarge didn't work Thursdays. That side of the shop faces west, and I couldn't get a clear picture of the man through the glare of the sun. He seemed to spontaneously emerge from a blast of yellow light. The shop had garage doors front and back, so anyone off the street could walk right in. The man moved tentatively, like a lost soul, and stopped in front of my dad's office. He appeared to have crawled from the bottom of a hamper and had the vacant look of a homeless person. The man was well over six feet tall, so I picked up a hammer just in case. The twenty-two ouncer. With the weight of it I could sink a sixteen-penny nail in three solid hits.

"Maybe he needs a cabinet for under the bridge," Juan said, just loud enough for me to hear over the table saw and the routers. Juan spoke with an accent and looked like he'd been living in the wild, with an explosion of black hair and four days of beard growth. He was a Cuban whose family was lucky enough to have drifted all the way to shore, somewhere near Key West. I laughed at his remark but didn't drop the hammer.

My dad came out of the office, looked up to the homeless man and engaged him in conversation. My dad, the fire hydrant. A thick Sicilian with a barrel chest and a kind, round face. The black man gestured and opened his hand. Dad stared at the ground as if concentrating on the man's words over the machinery, but I realized he was looking at the man's feet. It was cool, mid-fifties, and the man stood barefoot. Our shop was across the railroad tracks on the industrial side of Ybor City. If you didn't step on broken glass or screws or shred your feet on discarded metal, you'd likely step on a syringe.

Fausto stood behind the table saw cutting four by eight sheets of three-quarter inch particle board, producing clouds of sawdust that danced in the sunlight, permeated the air and stuck to our skin and our hair and became a part of us. He was oblivious to the visitor.

Dad motioned for the man to wait and this pissed me off. We were tight and until money came in there wasn't any to spare. Over the summer TECO had shut off the power because we hadn't paid the electric bill. Every month we teetered on disaster.

"If my old man gives this dude any money I'm going to blow a fuse," I said into Juan's ear, keeping a watchful eye on the beggar. "I haven't seen a penny in three weeks."

Del stood directly behind us routing the edges of the mica he'd just glued down. Juan laughed and glanced at Del who was spraying cuttings our direction.

My dad walked out of the office holding a pair of old leather work boots. The man was a packrat and kept all his old shoes piled under his desk. He dropped the pair of low-tops on the concrete and the man bent over and struggled to squeeze his hobbit feet into those size nines. Dad had extra wide feet, and a few toes missing on his right foot from his time in Korea, which gave him an odd gait when he walked. The man kicked off the shoes and gestured to my dad. The shoes didn't fit. They were plenty wide, but too short.

I leaned against the cabinet Juan and I had just assembled with my arms crossed. I didn't know why my dad didn't just wave this dude off. Some homeless drunk stumbled in begging for a handout every other week, not sure what made this guy any different.

"Roberto," Dad shouted in English. "Bring me the tinsnips."

I dropped the hammer and walked up front with the snips and handed them to my dad. I looked up to the man, who didn't seem as tall close-up, but was taller than me. We nodded at each other. His eyes looked ancient. He wore tattered, brown cotton pants and a faded Jimi Hendrix Purple Haze T-shirt so thin, you could see errant black chest hairs popping through it. His nappy hair was matted to one side and he had a scraggly beard. His eyes were bloodshot and tinged with yellow. He looked older than I originally thought and there were grays in his beard and hair. The man had been burned at one time in his life and that history was painfully apparent on one of his arms. The discolored skin looked like melted plastic that had welted and bubbled, then cooled in grotesque waves. He had a sour smell like someone who'd been sweating alcohol but seemed to be steady on his feet and didn't appear to be drunk. I backed away from him.

"You and Juan stack those units, so they don't get damaged," my dad said to me before turning his attention to the shoes. I nodded and went back to work, satisfied that the man was harmless.

Juan and I stacked the base unit with the others. It didn't have drawers or doors yet; those would get installed later when all the units were assembled. I kept looking toward the front of the shop to watch my dad work on those shoes with the tinsnips. He cut the top front part of the shoes away so the man's toes could stick out and he took his time doing it, like he was crafting a piece of art.

"My dad thinks he's a cobbler," I said to Juan, who shook his head.

The table saw wound down and Fausto rattled something off in Spanish to Juan who went to help him move the stacks of doors and drawer faces he'd cut. They moved the wood to the back of the shop for the night crew to laminate, while I gathered materials for the next cabinet. The varying decibels of machinery quieted, revealing Rush's "Tom Sawyer" squawking from the crappy shop radio, creating a soundtrack of sorts for this unfolding drama. I looked behind me at Del, who was squinting through his one good eye at my dad. Del was a gangly stoner with wavy blond hair who looked like a weathered version of an eighties rock star. He'd lost sight in one eye from a brawl he had the previous year and cocked his head to one side as if he were still getting used to it.

"Your old man likes to take in strays," he said.

"That how we found you?" I said.

"Pretty much," he said.

Now the homeless man sat with his ass on the concrete floor and my dad stood over him watching him struggle. The shoes still didn't fit. I glanced back at Del who was grinning. At this point, everyone in the shop was half watching and half working. The man handed the shoes back one at a time and my dad cut out the backs so they could be worn like slippers. The man put the shoes on his feet and smiled like he'd been fitted with Italian loafers. When he stood up, I could see that his toes hung off the fronts and his heals hung off the backs. I figured that was the end of our entertainment and this guy would be on his merry way. Their conversation continued and I wanted to smash something with a hammer. I wasn't even sure why.

"Robert," Juan said. "Let's get the next one going."

We assembled the next cabinet while my dad and the man engaged in conversation. My dad pointed into the shop and then turned and pointed out the front garage door toward the dumpster and I knew exactly what was up. This vagrant had just become our newest employee.

My dad handed him a broom and a flat shovel, and the man went to work sweeping the shop and throwing away the wood scraps piled beneath the saw, though he did put a few pieces aside. I imagined him and his homeless brethren gathered around a fifty-five-gallon drum burning the wood for warmth. He worked quietly, and though he glanced at each of us while working that broom and shovel, he shied away from eye contact and not a word was said. He had a delicate almost meticulous way about him that I couldn't wrap my head around. After sweeping the shop and throwing away the trash, which required a dozen or so trips to the dumpster, the man looked around, as if surveying the place for the first time, and then he put away the tools that weren't in use. There was a wall in the shop covered with tempered Masonite, where we hung the hand tools. When I was ten, I outlined all the tools in black marker, so we'd always know exactly where they went.

While I was on my knees popping staples into the back of a cabinet to square it up, I looked over to see the man in the boot slippers looking down at me. His thick, overgrown toenails looked like claws.

"Man, I'm thirsty as hell," he said to me. "Think I could have some water?"

I said there was a jug of cold water in the refrigerator and told him where to find the Styrofoam cups. His arm was hard to look at and equally hard not to, and I couldn't stop myself.

"Yeah man, I'm still putting out that fire," he said.

I watched him pour and drink five cups of water. When he finished, he nodded at me and walked to the front of the shop, knocked on the office door, then went in. I'd only worked a half day, because I had classes in the morning, but I was ready to get the hell out of there. I looked around at the shop. It was pristine. As clean as I'd seen it in a while, and I was relieved because it was one less thing I'd have to do.

Fausto went to work making the shop dirty again, cutting strips of sapele, a type of African mahogany to be used as inlays in a desk, and the shop filled with a sweet leathery scent and smelled alive. Sawdust sparkled in the afternoon light and everyone was in motion, routing, or filing, or cutting, or sanding, or cleaning, or stacking their work, while I stared out the door hating everything about this place.

"Roberto, *vieni qui*," my dad shouted and waved me toward the office. When I walked in, he was at his desk counting bills and placing them into envelopes. The homeless man was not there. The office was so crowded with wood and mica samples, blue prints and trade magazines there was hardly a place to stand, though there was a red seat next to the desk that had spongey yellow foam popping through cracks in the vinyl. Everything was covered with a fine layer of dust, even the pictures on the walls. On a bookshelf, three overstuffed photo albums bulged proudly with pictures of every cabinet we'd ever built, which for me, was like looking at photographs of strangers.

Dad paid everyone cash, which even then I knew was terrible business and I'd said as much to him more than once, and he'd always say, "I'm not giving Giuseppe a goddamned penny." Ten years earlier, the IRS had locked up the shop because he hadn't paid his taxes, after that, everyone from the IRS became Giuseppe Garibaldi.

"Count the money," Dad said. "Give everyone their envelope and tell them they'll get the rest next week."

We were going on eight months of this shit and as we got closer to the holidays, the undercurrent of frustration in the shop became a burden of weight that weakened the will and corrupted the soul. After delivering the thin envelopes to a reception of blank stares, I went back to the office to get my pay. Dad handed me a twenty and I looked at the bill as if it were counterfeit. "Twenty bucks?" I said and sunk. I always got hind tit, a perk of being the owner's son.

"I had sixty for you," he said, "but I didn't want you guys to stop working to clean up. I gave forty to Larry."

"Larry?" I said.

"The homeless guy," he said. "You'll survive until next week." Then a thought came to him and he smiled so big I could see his bridgework. "And that man, he works like a sonofabitch."

I wanted to punch a hole through the wall. "Now we're giving every beggar who stumbles in here a job?" I said. "We can't even pay ourselves."

He shook his head at me like I was a mistake, like I wasn't his son, like the time I got sent to the principal's office for cheating on a test in high school. "He didn't come in here begging," he said. "That man wanted work, and you never deny that of a man. You take that away and you steal his reason for being."

My cell phone vibrated at seven on Saturday and light through the faux wood blinds hurt my head. Dad wanted me to pick up café con leche and Cuban bread for the guys. I mumbled something that I'm sure was unintelligible, set the alarm for thirty minutes and put my head under the covers. I had blown through the twenty he'd given me, but didn't think of it in time, so I'd have to put the coffees on a credit card. When the alarm buzzed, I got up, put on a sweatshirt and a pair of jeans and drank two glasses of water with four ibuprofens. The place smelled like vomit, so I cracked the jalousie windows.

I'd gone out with my buddy Mike Harper the night before. We met two homely girls at a bar, one of whom Mike knew, and had, as he described, a morally loose disposition and big tits. The other girl, Jen, had a pear-shaped body and stared at me with guarded condescension while Mike and Beth, that was the busty girl's name, were laughing and had their hands on each other. I introduced myself and Jen announced that she had joined the Peace

Corps and was leaving for Costa Rica in two weeks. Her face was the planet earth with broad hills and valleys and life exploding from every pore. She had just arrived from Kansas having escaped farm life and born-again parents. She said she was homeless and crashing on her friend's couch. An hour later, Jen and I sat on opposing ends of that couch listening to Mike and Beth have sex in the bedroom. The bed creaked and every so often bumped the wall and I could hear the girl giggle. I imagined their tangled bodies flopping around. I was a little drunk and a lot horny and given the chance I'd of jumped on Jen, homely or not. She might have suspected as much, because when I looked over she seemed to be writhing in pain.

"We deserve to be rewarded for this," I announced, and went to the kitchenette to rummage through the cabinets for more alcohol. I hit pay dirt in the refrigerator. Tucked in the back, I found a bottle of Moët & Chandon. When I pulled it out, Jen's eyes bugged-out, which led me to believe that it was something of value, and less likely to give me a hangover.

"She's saving that," Jen said as I untwisted the wire over the cork. "It's expensive."

I popped it open and said Happy New Year.

We turned on the television, drank champagne from juice glasses and watched part of an old Brando flick with a gang on motorcycles tearing up a town.

Mike walked out of the bedroom at two in the morning looking like he'd won a stuffed animal at the state fair. Jen was passed-out and the room was rocking like one of those rope bridges. Mike held his shoes in one hand and put a finger to his lips indicating that we were sneaking out. I looked at Mike's feet and could see his white skin through the holes in his black socks. When we got to his car, I threw up in the parking lot and then once more on the drive home. I don't remember anything after that.

I picked up the bread and coffees and arrived at the shop with a hammer slamming inside my skull. Thankfully the place was quiet, though the guys were laughing about something and their voices drifted in the air with the sawdust.

"You went back to sleep," my dad said, and snatched the box out of my hands. I must have looked like shit too because he turned back and said, "And don't get near that goddamned table saw until your head is screwed on right." I grabbed one of the coffees out of the box before he turned and walked it over to the boys.

COMETS

The homeless man stood near the other guys, but not with them. He wore a cream-colored guayabera, frayed at the edges, and he stood there crabbing in gray cotton pants with black Converse All Stars on his feet. High tops. His hair was shorter than it had been two days earlier. He still looked homeless. Something about the age and wear of clothes that didn't fit and didn't match. I looked down at those worn Chucks and could see his black skin through holes in the canvas.

The guys were listening to Crazy Jimmy explain how he'd won a couple hundred dollars on his pigeons. Jimmy talked to himself a lot and always wore long sleeves, even in the summer heat. He trained homing pigeons, I guess you could call them, and entered competitions where they'd put money in a pool and drive hundreds of miles to release the birds. You'd win money based on whose pigeons arrived home first.

"Pigeons are nasty birds," Larry said, and the guys turned toward him. "They're greasy and chew like gristle." No one quite knew what to say to this.

"Eat up," my dad interjected, "we got work to do."

The boys dug into the food. Larry watched them with hands in his pockets.

"Larry, get some coffee and toast," my dad said. "It's café con leche. It'll put lead in your pencil and hair on your chest."

"My pencil got plenty of lead, Johnny," Larry said, helping himself.

"Margie made me get snipped," Crazy Jimmy said. "Now I got unleaded." We all laughed at that.

Larry turned to me and nodded, probably because I was staring at him.

"Larry, this is Roberto," Dad said. "My son."

"Roberto," Larry said, rolling the R in my name with the exuberance of a Spanish soccer commentator. "*Es un gran placer conocerte.*"

"*Tu hablas español.*" Dad rattled off to Larry in Spanish.

"Man, I speak a little bit of everything, Spanish, Italian, French."

"That's the greatest," Dad said, adding this man to his collection. Then he told me to teach Larry how to glue and route and there was no getting out of it.

I explained the compressor and the glue pot and the optimum pressure for spraying and we went to work laminating four-by-eight sheets of mica onto high density particle board. He picked it all up quickly. When I explained the part about rolling and routing, Larry shouted, "Roll'em and rob'em? What kind of shop y'all runnin' over here?" The whole place burst out laughing.

Larry didn't smell bad, though he was sweating something thick. But the skin on the burned arm didn't sweat.

"You got shoes," I said.

"Johnny paid me on Thursday. I went up to the Salvation Army and got fixed up. New clothes, haircut, shower, hot meal and a bunk for the night. They don't take you if they know you're drunk."

"That how you lost your shoes?" I said.

"I drink," he said, with a blank stare. "That's the marrow of the bone."

I didn't understand what he meant by that. Larry put in a full day and he worked hard as hell and he was still there in the evening when I left.

I stayed home that night. My apartment was above a garage in an historic area called Seminole Heights. The walls were covered in ancient, tongue-and-groove cedar and the place smelled like it had a memory, like it held onto some part of every person who'd found refuge here. And I knew that when I left, it would hold onto a piece of me.

I took a hot shower and had a beer and as the temperature fell outside, I looked into the darkness and thought about Larry. I wondered if he was out there in his paper thin, Cuban shirt and barefooted inside his All Stars. I wondered what he ate for dinner and if he was drinking. I wondered how anyone ends up where they end up, and where I would be when I was his age.

"When was the last time you went to confession?" my mother said. She stood behind me pulling meatballs out of red sauce and placing them on a serving dish while I stared into a refrigerator so full it was hard to find anything. I didn't respond.

"That's what I thought," she said, snapping lids on the pots as if to punctuate her disappointment. "Monsignor asked about you this morning."

"Where's the wine?" I asked, stuffing a piece of prosciutto in my mouth.

"On the table," she said.

The woman made sauce from scratch every Sunday, as her mother did before her, and she wasn't happy that I'd stopped coming by to eat. Which, coincidently, was the same time I stopped going to church. I poured myself a glass of wine

17

and set the table for three and Mom said to put an extra dish. I didn't think anything of that. You never knew who might show up to eat. We'd had all the guys over at one time or another.

The front door opened and shut, and without looking, Mom sang out, "Go wash up. Everything's ready." She was bent over, staring into the oven. From the kitchen table I watched my dad and Larry walk in and my eyes widened a bit. Bringing Larry home was bold, even for my dad, and it made me uncomfortable.

"Larry, we're going to turn you into an Italian today," Dad said bursting into the kitchen. "Rose, this is Larry," Dad announced. "He speaks four languages."

Larry wore the same ill-fitting clothes, but the guayabera looked like he'd rolled in dirt and his lopsided hair had sawdust in it. Mom stared at Larry, wringing her hands in her apron.

"Pleased to meet you Ma'am," Larry said, and he smiled with bad teeth. "Been a long time since I ate home cookin'." Larry shifted his weight uncomfortably under Mom's scrutiny.

"Go wash yourself," she said. Her face flushed red. "The bathroom is down the hall." Larry nodded like a schoolboy. Then she said, "John," and walked into the living room. Dad shot me a look like this was my doing. They'd been married a lifetime, and as far as I could tell had bickered from the moment they said I do. Their generation stuck it out to the end.

I sipped wine and eavesdropped as she berated my Dad in Italian. Who was this man? Where did he come from? Was he going to come back and steal everything in the house? He looked at my Lladrós. He's going to dirty my towels. Those people, they carry disease. Mom stopped talking momentarily and nodded when Larry walked by. He made a beeline toward me. I stood near the kitchen table eating cheese and crackers and drinking my wine.

"Stunod!" my mother's voice echoed from the other room.

Larry chuckled upon hearing the word. "You never been married," he said.

I shook my head and said, "Help yourself to some cheese and crackers." But Larry had no interest in appetizers. He stared at my wine as if it were a puzzle, licked his lips and turned toward the three remaining glasses and the cheap wicker-wrapped bottle of Chianti on the table. He poured a glass, a fat pour like mine. He emptied half the glass in the first swallow and poured himself more.

"That'll set things right," he said and smiled at me, which gave me a sickly feeling in my gut.

Dad walked in and went directly to the table and grabbed the wine bottle. "No wine today," he announced. "We got a job to deliver this afternoon." He reached for Larry's wine glass, but Larry held it away and held his ground.

"If y'all gonna drink wine, I'm drinkin' with you," Larry said.

"We're not drinking wine," my dad said and shot me a look as if Larry's temptations were on me.

I set my wine glass on the kitchen counter and slid it away.

Dad stood his ground and held his hand out. "Larry, you don't need that."

"I'm gonna drink this wine, Johnny," Larry said quietly.

I didn't like the look in Larry's eyes. A door closed in the other room and the floor creaked as Mom marched toward the kitchen.

"Just the one, Johnny," Larry said, in a pleading whisper. "Just the one."

Mom walked in the room and Dad relaxed his posture, and I realized I'd been holding my breath. Dad turned away from Larry and put the bottle on the kitchen counter.

"I would like a glass of wine, John," Mom said, oblivious to the standoff. She poured a glass and placed the bottle on the table. "What's gotten into you?"

Larry raised his glass and said, "*Salute cent' anni.*"

I left my glass of wine on the counter and sat at the table. When we were seated, my mother blessed herself and prayed. Larry, Dad, and I stared at her with our heads bowed. When she looked up, we dug in.

Larry sipped his wine and true to his word, didn't pour anymore. He did a lot of talking. Said he'd been in the service and lived in New Orleans and had worked a lot of odd jobs. He had traveled through Europe and was there long enough to learn the languages. The man was a puzzle. How could he be where he is having been where he's been and not want more?

My mom stuffed four containers of leftovers in a grocery bag and handed the bag to Larry on his way out the door. As soon as Larry and my father were gone, she grabbed all the towels from the bathroom, walked them into the laundry room and mumbled, "*Brutto comme la fame.*" He was ugly as hunger.

I drank the rest of my wine and poured another glass.

"Where's your protégé?" I asked my dad on Monday afternoon when I got to the shop. He shook his head and said that Larry wasn't at the Salvation Army when he went to pick him up.

"I dropped him off last night, but I guess he never went inside," he said pointing at a pile of drawers. He said to start installing the tracks and left to see about a couple of new jobs.

We were building workstations for a beauty shop owned by Mr. Lewis King in Sarasota. Mr. Lewis, as my dad called him, was a nice man, but his wife was a jackal. We'd installed half a dozen beauty shops for Mr. Lewis and were a few weeks late on the newest installation. My dad had taken Larry down to Sarasota on Sunday to make a small delivery and get another draw on the job and that worked out fine, because I finally got a decent chunk of pay.

Larry didn't show Monday or Tuesday and the place was back to normal. On Wednesday, we accidently killed a chicken. There were chickens all over Ybor City, brought here by the Cubans who rolled cigars at the turn of the century. One walked in the shop right after lunch, and we all threw a buck on one of the work tables to see who could catch it. My dad wasn't there. Del, Crazy Jimmy, Juan, and I were in the pool. Sarge didn't want anything to do with it. Fausto, who had ill-fitting dentures and always appeared to be smiling, folded his arms and watched us chase the chicken around the shop and slide on the sawdust which covered the slick concrete floor. Crazy Jimmy, skinny as a ferret and about my height, rounded a corner and both his feet came out from under him just as the chicken went through his legs. He crushed the bird with his ass. It made a quick squawk and a low crunch.

"*Dios mío*," Jimmy said. "I kilt the chicken. I kilt the chicken." I helped him up from the floor and he dusted himself off. He looked at the chicken quivering on the ground with blood seeping from its beak and he walked outside and bent over at the waist like a hinge, then stood there talking to himself.

I stuffed the four dollars in Jimmy's hand and grabbed the shovel. The guys were cracking chicken dinner jokes and Fausto mimicked the bird's last croak with a gummy smile on his face. I buried the bird in the place where all sins reside, just below the surface, and the shop was back to normal when Dad arrived.

That afternoon, Larry walked in. He wavered in the open garage door, backlit by the sun. A black figure growing from a ball of white light. As he came into the shop and into focus, I could see his mouth hung open and his body fighting to hold balance. This wasn't Larry the worker or Larry the linguist. It was Larry the drunk. The guys were working, but one by one they turned to see what drew my attention.

"I got this," Sarge said, walking by me. "I was an MP. Dealt with this kind of shit all the time."

"That's Larry," I said. Sarge stopped and turned toward me wide-eyed. He had not met Larry yet.

"What're you muthafuckas lookin' at?" Larry blurted out. "I'm here build me some cab-nets. We gone roll'em and we gone rob'em. Hey, hey, hey, and y'all gotta brother working for you." Larry pointed at Sarge. "The fuck you lookin' at? You ain't no better'n me, nigger."

About that time, Dad rushed out of the office and put his hand on Larry's shoulder, gently, as if greeting an old friend. Larry spun and pushed my father's hand away. I grabbed the hammer and walked toward the front of the shop.

"You owe me money, Johnny," Larry said.

"He puts a hand on your daddy, I'm gonna break him in half," Sarge said, walking with me.

"Go back to work," my dad said as smooth as butter. "It's okay."

"Yeah," Larry shouted. "Git on back to it. I ain't scared of you."

Larry took a step toward us and Dad put a hand behind one of Larry's arms and said, "Larry, let's go talk out here. I know I owe you money. Hell, I owe everybody money." Larry turned and moved with him toward the garage door. I wanted to hear the conversation, but they were too far away. They stood outside for ten minutes, then Larry climbed in the passenger seat of our van. Dad walked in the office and walked out with the keys. I watched them drive off and thought about something Brando said in that motorcycle movie, when asked what he was rebelling against. He said, "Whaddya got?" Yeah, I thought. Whaddya got?

When I arrived on Saturday morning, the guys were loading the truck and trailer for the trip to Sarasota. We were going to deliver the beauty shop to Mr. Lewis. I walked in the shop and saw Larry's grocery cart full of junk parked inside the garage door and looked at the stuff it contained; a rolled-up tent, an old wool blanket, a puffy blue jacket, grease stained and losing its stuffing, a can of Campbell's soup, a green extension cord, pencils and pens bound by a pipe cleaner, a couple of coverless books that were bloated from having gotten wet, and a little wooden club, the kind cops used to carry.

"Yeah, man," Larry said as I eyed his cart, "I'm a turtle in this life. I carry it all with me and it's heavy. So, goddamned heavy."

It was mid-November and in the low 70s. A chamber of commerce day. Larry had been with us for about six weeks and had fallen off the wagon three times, that we knew of. He'd disappear for a few days, then come back as if it were nothing out of the ordinary. Larry had become a part-time employee and worked hard when he showed, though his work schedule remained a mystery to all of us, including my dad. We'd all gotten used to his presence, and when he came into work, he was one of the guys.

Larry and I rode to Sarasota with my dad, who drove the van. Larry sat in the passenger seat, and I sat just behind the two seats on a packing blanket which I'd thrown over the toolbox. Larry and Dad talked the whole way down, in multiple languages.

Del and Crazy Jimmy followed us in a faded green station wagon that burned oil and blew smoke from the tail pipe. The station wagon held Crazy Jimmy's pigeons. He wanted to release the birds from Sarasota as a training run.

"It was cold last night," my dad said to Larry. "Where'd you sleep?"

"I got me a friend. She lets me stay with her sometimes, but she charges me."

"So, you do have lead in your pencil," my dad said.

"I am a soldier, Johnny" Larry said, and he and my dad laughed.

When we arrived, my dad divvied up the duties. The existing beauty shop catered to the blue hairs and needed a facelift. Our job was to remove the old units as gently as possible, so Mr. Lewis could resell them, but Mr. Lewis never showed. He sent his wife, Mrs. King. We turned off the water and disconnected the plumbing while she watched us like a prison guard. The woman sucked on Pall Malls the entire day and barked at us with smoky breath as if the fires of hell were burning inside her. Wiry and wrinkly with black roots propping up an explosion of bleached hair, she seemed to bristle at our presence. She'd driven up in a big fat hog Mercedes and reeked of money. We'd put a kitchen in their home a few years earlier and when we got there to install, there were dirty dishes in the sink and the cabinets were full. You'd never get that from an old Cuban or Sicilian woman in West Tampa. The kitchen would be spotless and the cabinets empty.

I overheard her whisper to my dad that she didn't want *him*, speaking of Larry, left alone in the building. "I don't trust *his* type," she said.

"Don't worry about Larry," Dad said to her. "He's one of my boys."

Larry stood out as different and different wasn't to be trusted.

We were prying loose a unit and Larry asked for the hammer. I handed it to him, and he felt the weight of it. "Man, I could use a hammer like this," he said.

"I'll bet," I said. "Living on the streets is dangerous."

He chuckled and said he had a tent and would use the hammer to drive stakes in the ground.

"If you worked a regular schedule, you could probably afford a place to live," I said.

"Man, I don't need no anchors in my life," he said with conviction. "When that anchor goes, you sink fast."

We loaded up the old units with far more care than they deserved. We should have been making a trip to the dump, but instead, we headed across town to store them. Under Mrs. King's watchful eye, we placed the old units in a cavernous warehouse stacked full of shampoos and rinses and chemicals, old furniture, beauty and barber chairs, and other mysterious salon equipment. We finished loading in all the old units and walked out as a group, but Larry was not among us.

"Where's the other one?" Mrs. King said. Then she leaned toward my dad and said, "I told you that nigger was no good. He's going to steal something."

"Don't talk about my boys that way," Dad said to her.

Mrs. King bee-lined into the warehouse and we followed.

Piano music echoed softly in the warehouse and for a moment, we all looked at one another curiously, except for Mrs. King, who marched with purpose deeper into the building. We rounded a set of large boxes and there sat Larry, behind an aged baby grand. His eyes were closed, and his hands floated softly over the keys. I want to say that it was jazz; the kind you might hear late at night in jazz club, but I wasn't sure. It seemed like improvisation. We stopped and watched Larry play and the music nourished us, connected us and lifted us from that place. We were transported by his passion. Even Mrs. King, held her poison.

Everyone stood back, still as ghosts, but I couldn't. I walked to the piano and watched him, and I could tell the music, that was sweet and melancholy, came from deep inside him. A place no one could touch. When he finished and opened his eyes, they were filled with water, but I didn't see sadness there.

"It's for sale if you want it," Mrs. King said. "If not, cover it up. I've got to lock the place up." She turned and walked out.

Larry gently closed the keyboard cover and pulled Visqueen over the piano. "I had one like this," he said to me. "She was a beauty, but she burned. They all burned." He pursed his lips and walked toward the burst of sunlight that flooded through the door. Del patted Larry on the back, and we all walked out.

After Mrs. King drove away, Crazy Jimmy opened the cage in the back of his station wagon, tagged his birds and released them one at a time. There were a dozen birds in all. Rock doves, he called them. The five of us looked up into a great big blue sky filled with puffy white clouds and we watched those birds scatter. Some of them flew out of sight with no fear of losing their way, while others perched in treetops, perhaps to get their bearings.

"Do they all find their way home?" Larry asked.

Crazy Jimmy said, "No. Sometimes they lose their way and never make it back."

I looked up and imagined myself as one of those birds, unanchored, looking down on this group of men, and I focused on Larry the homeless man and Larry the linguist, one of Johnny's boys, who was ugly as hunger and Mrs. King's nigger, and who cried music from a broken place, and I struggled to get my bearings.

I parked the van in the street, locked it, walked into the Salvation Army and froze in a hallway wondering where to go. The place smelled thick, like the wrestling locker room from high school. The parquet floors were dull, and the varnish worn away from thousands of people who had shuffled over them. There were offices on either side of a hall that opened to a large room with dozens of cots.

My dad had sent me to pick up materials for a job but said to find Larry and give him his money. We hadn't seen Larry in several weeks. In my pocket there was a hundred and fifty bucks cash stuffed in an envelope. A gray man in his fifties rolled a galvanized bucket and mop into the hall and stopped when he saw me. The man was clean and freshly shaven, but he wore clothes that didn't quite fit and didn't quite match with black shoes that had Velcro straps. He said Larry hadn't been around, but I might be able to find him at the Platt Street Bridge.

"He's probably on a bender," the man said, "and if he is, I wouldn't go there."

I went to the supply house and picked up wood, rolls of mica, staples, and five-gallon buckets of Hybond-80, this pungent glue for laminating, then I drove through downtown and stopped by the bridge to see if I could find Larry. Traffic was gridlocked and snaked along Bayshore Boulevard creating an endless line of headlights. I parked for a few minutes and watched but didn't see anyone in the fading light. It wasn't the best part of town and I was hesitant to look, but something drew me under that bridge.

The sound of traffic created a cadence that echoed overhead and mimicked the pulse in my chest. Through the dull light, I saw Larry's grocery cart with Larry sprawled on the ground next to it. My hand gripped a utility knife with the blade extended. I took shallow breaths and cringed. I expected the stench of urine, but this was more than that and Larry's pants were wet with it.

"Larry," I shouted. He screamed something that wasn't language and swung at me from the ground with the little wooden club. The light was dim, but I could see his face was bloodied. I shouted his name again and he swung at me again. My stomach turned and I left him there on the ground.

The sun was setting now, a fiery ball of orange casting hues of pink into the western clouds. I sat in the van with my hands wet on the steering wheel staring at nothing and I thought about what Crazy Jimmy had said. Sometimes they never make it back. I jumped out of the van and dug into our toolbox. Back under the bridge, I stood at Larry's feet holding the 22-ounce hammer. I watched him for a moment, tucked the hammer into his grocery cart and walked away.

JOSEPH ALLEN COSTA

Fly Away Home

Crazy Jimmy kept birds and walked around with bags under busy eyes that kept watch for the boy. A bony, vascular man with black, receding hair, his clothes hung on him like a scarecrow that had the stuffing beaten out of it.

His wife, Margie, had dry mouth and drank water all night, peed a lot and read the Holy Bible during bouts of insomnia. Jimmy was a light sleeper, but when he slept, he dreamed of flying with his birds. Flying not like a bird, or a superhero, but treading his feet as if through water. In his imaginings, he would jump and kick hard and glide slowly behind his pigeons, he called them rock doves, but always struggled to keep up. When he fell behind, he'd use his arms to propel himself faster. If he stopped kicking, even for a moment, he would sink and be startled awake before he touched the ground. He wished to have that dream every night. He wished to be lighter than air. He wished to catch those pigeons and show them the way home.

Jimmy bobbed and jabbed the air, ducked, then raised his hands and did a little dance around the imaginary ring, even though there was no ring, just a makeshift shed with an uneven floor made from old pallets, scraps of plywood, and a rusted tin roof that covered a dozen pigeons who watched Jimmy and cooed from their cage. He punched the air and thought about the money he could make in the Summer Classic pigeon race.

The rock doves were a mix of colors: a mix of white, brown, gray, and black. They cooed and jostled in their six-foot cage while Jimmy shadow boxed and spoke to them with beads of sweat rolling into his eyes and burning. He called each one by name: Horse, Lulu, Mr. President, Sugar Ray, Roberto Durán, and Johnny.

Johnny was a stout brown bird that reminded him of the fireplug Sicilian with the cabinet shop in Tampa. The bird was industrious, always busy, and always came in dead last. Jimmy built cabinets out of his garage but had learned the trade working for Johnny and still worked for him now and again. Jimmy went into business for himself when he and Margie bought the five acres of land in Dade City, off Highway 54. It was a place they would never leave, could never leave.

The birds knew this to be home. No matter where Jimmy drove to set them free, they found their way back here. Every so often, a bird would go missing while the others returned. Sometimes the missing bird would show up weeks or months after the others, and other times the bird never came back. The reason remained a mystery. Sometimes birds lose their way or have an accident. Sometimes they become victims of predators.

"That's right, Horse," Jimmy said to his breadwinner, jabbing the air, moving, ducking, and then a quick jab, cross, uppercut. "You gonna be my workhorse? How 'bout you Lulu? Oye Roberto, you gonna fly and win me some cold-motherfucking-cash or you gonna fight Sugar Ray again?" The two birds didn't get along. They once went at each other pecking and clawing, leaving a wreckage of feathers and smears of blood in the cage.

"She would be mad at you for using bad words," the boy said, watching Jimmy.

Jimmy spun around, startled. "I didn't know you were there."

The skinny boy had pin straight, black hair, hazel eyes, and olive skin. He wore a red cotton T-shirt, blue jeans, and dingy, white Converse All Stars.

"Let's not tell her," Jimmy said, wiping the glisten of sweat from his forehead and rubbing his wet palms on his jeans. Jimmy had come out at sunrise to attend his birds and to be there for the boy. He wanted to be everything a real father should be. Though still early, the sun was well above the horizon and through the walls of the loosely constructed bird coop a luminous shaft illuminated the boy in heavenly light.

"Were you a good boxer?" the boy said.

"What do you think?" Jimmy said, bobbing his head like a fighter and throwing more jabs.

The boy smiled and hooked his thumbs into his bulging front pockets. Whatever was hidden away in them was lumpy, like they were full of beans. Jimmy looked at the boy's pockets. The boy had secrets and Jimmy had become accustomed to that. But the longer he looked at those pockets, the clearer the secret became, until at once, it was no longer a secret but a profound memory.

Jimmy grabbed a measuring cup that hung on a rusty nail and scooped birdfeed from a forty-pound bag while the boy watched. He opened the cage and poured food into a communal trough, caressing each bird and talking sweetly to them. Seeing the food, the birds cooed and flapped their wings and pecked and scratched, making a racket as they vied for position and ate with gusto.

The boy focused on the jagged, vertical scars that ran along the inside of Jimmy's wrists. Jimmy tugged at the sleeves of his denim shirt.

"Do they know their names?" the boy said.

Jimmy addressed the gray rock dove that had its head held high as if it were better than the others. "*¿Qué es su nombre?*" he asked and then responded, "*El Presidente*," in a falsetto voice.

The boy laughed and Jimmy smiled, rubbed his eyes and fought back a yawn. Margie had been up a better part of the night while Jimmy lay in bed with his hands on his chest like a corpse, listening to her pray quietly in the living room and thinking about the date on the calendar and what it meant. Margie prayed the rosary, repeating the Apostle's Creed, the Lord's Prayer, the Hail Mary, and Glory Be until it became white noise. She recited bible passages, and one in particular stood out, one Jimmy knew to be her favorite. "Whoever receives one such child in my name receives me; and whoever receives me, receives not me but him who sent me."

"You don't pray like she does," the boy said.

"I don't need to pray like her," Jimmy said. "She's missing something."

"What's she missing?"

Jimmy stared at the boy. He walked past the boy, who stood just inside the shed, and he peered toward the house. Margie often sat on the front porch in the mornings sipping coffee and staring at the winding shell driveway that led from the main road.

"She's in the flower garden," the boy said. "She does that this time of year. They're for today."

Jimmy understood the significance of the day, but he had other plans and somehow the boy knew this.

"You're not going with her," the boy said.

Jimmy shook his head.

"She'll be mad about that."

Jimmy's father never married his mother. When he was twelve, Jimmy had a chance encounter with the man at a Golden Gloves competition. The man was there with a boy who bore an uncanny resemblance to Jimmy. Having been told by his mother who the man was, Jimmy approached him. The man took him aside, poked a finger in his chest, called him a bastard liar and said his mother was a whore. Jimmy fought his half-brother that day and was disqualified after splitting the boy's nose open and beating him down to the canvas well after the bell. Jimmy bloodied the boy's face until it no longer resembled his own.

Jimmy became the Ybor City welterweight, Golden Gloves runner up at seventeen. To psyche himself up for matches he would punch himself in the face and curse at his opponents in Spanish, which earned him the nickname Crazy Jimmy. Before his championship match, Jimmy punched himself so hard that he broke his own nose, which bled so badly the match was forfeited.

There was purity and punishment to fighting and a release valve for Jimmy at the end of his fists. But when Margie asked Jimmy to stop for her, for their future, he did, though he continued to visit the gym and hit the bag when he needed to.

Twenty-five years on, Jimmy had no illusions that he could still fight, at least not another person. Scabs on the knuckles of his hands were evidence of that, and of the battle with a wall that would not give.

Jimmy stood at the kitchen counter staring at the brewing coffee pot as if he could will it to happen faster. His eyes rose slowly toward a framed drawing that held a prominent place on the wall. The drawing was the face of a bright yellow sunflower, with the hint of a green stalk jutting up from the bottom of the frame. The flower was drawn with crayon on a white sheet of paper. In neat block letters, Mateo was written in brown on the top left side. Jimmy made the pine frame himself and stained it the same brown color as the center of the sunflower, knowing the boy would appreciate it. The boy had a great eye for detail. The boy. Jimmy couldn't bring himself to say his name. He thought that if he did, he would shatter into a million pieces like a fighter made of glass.

Margie walked in from outside as Jimmy made their coffees. His black, and Margie's with cream and one teaspoon of sugar. She put a hand to Jimmy's cheek, and he studied her once beautiful face, tired now and losing the battle to gravity. Her wavy brown hair, up in a ponytail, flecked with gray. Hazel eyes framed by crow's feet from reading the small type in her worn bible.

Jimmy thought about the way it used to be. The way Margie used to be. Funny, horny, and they were good together. Music, any music, would start her ass shaking. And she could move. That was the Cuban in her. When they married, there wasn't even a bible in the house.

"I heard you talking to your birds this morning," she said.

Jimmy nodded. "You were watering?"

"They're beautiful this year. Twelve feet tall. Mateo would be so proud." She held her coffee cup with both hands and looked at the scabs on Jimmy's knuckles. "You're coming with me today," she said in a manner that was more asking than telling.

"Margie, it's been ten years," Jimmy said, thinking of the boy, who never aged.

"I don't care how long it's been," she raised her voice.

"There's no one there, Margie. He's not there. He's not there."

Composing herself, she whispered, "I need a place to go. I need a place to be. It's his birthday."

Margie prayed and went to church and tended her flowers, the boy's flowers, and stared at that damned driveway. And Jimmy punched walls and released his pigeons and each time longed for their safe return.

"I'm going to release my birds in Ocala," he said. "It's the Summer Classic."

Margie's face turned red as pressure built inside her.

"He loves them," Jimmy said, then caught himself. "The birds. He loved to watch them fly. Come with me." Jimmy reached for her hand. Margie put her coffee on the counter and stepped close to Jimmy to feel his warmth.

"Come outside with me and sit," she said, looking at the sunflower drawing.

They walked to the backyard with their coffees, toward lawn furniture that faced a concentrated grove of sunflowers, twenty maybe thirty in all, packed tightly together. Bright faces of yellow and brown smiling toward the sky and held to the earth by thick green stalks.

"Mateo would walk around with sunflower seeds bulging in his front pockets, so he could secretly plant them," Margie said, watching the flowers, crinkling her eyes and smiling. "He loved his sunflowers."

"The seeds," Jimmy said as the memory blossomed. "I used to tell him he could grow his own little grove of sunflowers right out of his pockets." Jimmy looked deep into the sunflowers and saw the boy staring blankly at him. Then he looked to his wife and wondered how she summoned such strength.

Jimmy groaned a bit when his sore back hit the chair, and he thought about Roberto, Johnny's kid. A chicken had walked into the cabinet shop in Ybor City and Roberto goaded everyone into putting up a dollar to see who could catch it. Jimmy won when he slipped on sawdust that covered the slick concrete floor and he crushed the bird. Jimmy got a queasy stomach and was embarrassed at having to walk outside and bend over like a hinge with his hands on his knees and the boy watching him. Jimmy often looked at Roberto and wondered what his boy would have been like at twenty years old. The boys were the same age.

Jimmy had thought of that day a thousand times, but some mysteries weren't meant to be understood. Margie said she could see the school bus drive by in the distance and other cars as well. She waited for Mateo to turn the corner and run up the driveway as he always did, and she listened to Jimmy's table saw screaming from the garage, but the boy never came. Jimmy should have been there to meet him. He knew someone should have been there to meet him. That's what any good father would have done.

The bus had come and gone, and Mateo was two feet from the edge of his driveway when something caught his eye. He was a curious boy with a quick and crooked smile. Mateo turned away from the faint sound of his father's table saw and moved toward a sunflower just beyond the bus stop. One of his sunflowers. One that he had planted and nourished with water from his lunchbox. Mateo ran to the flower and dropped to his knees. He cleared away grass and weeds to ensure that the flower would thrive. He was so excited and focused on his accomplishment that he didn't hear the car pull over on the side of the road. He didn't hear the footsteps in the grass. He didn't notice the shadow that fell over him before the light was snatched away.

"Come with me to Ocala," Jimmy said. "I'm supposed to release the birds at ten o'clock this morning, if we leave now we can just make it and then I'll go with you this afternoon. We'll go together. I promise." Jimmy had only been to the cemetery once and decided on that day, he would not go back. The ground was empty, the boy was not there, and if the boy was not there, he was somewhere else.

Jimmy loaded the portable bird cage into the back of the station wagon and carried the birds one by one from the shed to the car. Out of the driveway, he turned onto Highway 54 and headed toward I-75, which would take them north to Ocala. Warm air blew through the open windows easing the gamey bird smell and carrying with it a stray tail feather which flittered through the car like a little white ghost. They drove in silence at first, both looking up at a deep blue sky with a few puffy white clouds. As they drove toward the interstate, Margie and Jimmy turned, almost in unison, toward the large property being cleared by bulldozers and tractors. The pines and oaks that once lined the highway were gone, sacrificed for progress.

"That was a beautiful piece of land," Jimmy said.

Margie nodded as if she agreed but also as if she didn't care one way or the other.

"I heard the guy who sold it had it for thirty years," Jimmy said. "Sold it for millions. It's going to be a shopping mall."

Before they reached the end of the property, just two miles down from their own, something else caught their attention and Jimmy tapped the brake. Margie and Jimmy exchanged looks, and Jimmy pulled the car over to the side of the road, his stomach turning in knots. The bulldozers had stopped moving and the workmen were gathered around a curious sight. In the middle of an open field, that was now just dirt and fallen trees, there stood a concentrated little grove of sunflowers, thirty or forty in all, packed tightly together standing twelve to fourteen feet tall. However, the men were not looking up at the sunflowers to marvel at their broad, bright faces, but instead, were staring at a singular spot on the ground. Each man's face a dismal mask.

"Please go, Jimmy," Margie said urgently. "Go now." Margie's hands were tightly weaved together and her lips were quietly moving in prayer.

Jimmy took one last look at the sunflowers and pulled on to Highway 54 with his mind racing. It can't be. He looked in the rearview mirror at the boy who sat quietly staring out the window with the sun shining on his face and Jimmy was comforted. Margie asked what he was looking at and Jimmy said nothing. The boy's presence was not his to share. They turned onto I-75 and Jimmy felt the urge to engage Margie in conversation, but he knew her mind was at work trying to reconcile the sunflowers, as was his, so he remained quiet for the duration.

Jimmy pulled his station wagon past a large banner that read, Central Florida Pigeon Club Summer Classic. He could see Margie's eyes open wide at the zoo of people and vehicles that packed the area. A woman wearing an orange vest waved them toward a parking spot. It was the first time Jimmy had brought Margie to a race.

Margie waited solemnly by the car, ringing her hands together, as Jimmy paid his entrance fee and exchanged pleasantries with the race officials, whom he knew from previous races. Jimmy walked back to the car with one of the officials who affixed an aluminum band to each of the pigeons. Upon each bird's arrival back in Dade City, Jimmy would remove the bands and place each one in a lockbox that recorded the time of arrival. Money was won based on a ratio of distance and airspeed, if the birds made it back.

Jimmy opened the back of the station wagon, which excited and agitated the birds. A few of the birds flew toward the cage door, while the others continued to peck at grain that Jimmy had tossed in the cage to keep them occupied. When Jimmy swung the cage door open, Horse and some of the more eager birds, took to the sky. He prodded the others out and they flew toward a white and wispy, cotton candy cloud, that to Jimmy resembled an old man with an unruly beard. They stood together, Jimmy and Margie, watching the birds shrink from sight.

Jimmy looked around for the boy, but Mateo was nowhere in sight. He was certain Mateo would be present for the release and felt himself growing anxious. Jimmy turned to the sky and watched one pigeon separate from the others. He took two steps forward and reached to the sky with both his hands. In his heart, Jimmy knew something profound had been lost and he felt the familiar urge to fly away, to forsake the ground.

JOSEPH ALLEN COSTA

TRAFFIC

Late afternoon and between shifts, the shop was as still as an empty church. The saw and the big fans were silent, the compressor quietly hissed, and the sun cast yellow shafts across the work floor, revealing an infinity of wood specks coruscating in the light. In the dampness of summer, the sawdust stuck to our skin and to our clothes and we'd taste it gritty in our mouths and breathe it into our lungs until it was a part of us. The air had an organic, leathery scent. I recall as a boy, sitting in this same spot with my grandfather, watching wood dance in the light and him saying that they were magic pieces of stardust. But this place never held any magic for me and if it did, I never opened my eyes wide enough to see it.

I slid the tongue-and-groove bottom of the next drawer into place to square up the dovetails, shot in a few staples, wiped away the excess glue with a damp cloth and stacked it with twenty-three others of varying sizes. At one time this might have been a skill, but now it seemed as rote as cutting grass. My hands ached and I sat on one of our low worktables. At the front of the shop my dad bowed over blueprints with a protractor, a note pad, and a Cuban cigar clenched in his teeth. A column of smoldering ash fell on the plans and he snatched them up quickly and shook them. A fat man dancing.

Pernell Grant walked in the shop. He spoke to my dad briefly and they shared a laugh, then he ambled back toward me with his thermos and a vintage lunch box shaped like a skinny Quonset hut. Pernell's size and constitution dictated he bring two sandwiches to eat each night. I grabbed a ceramic mug and blew the sawdust out of it and hit him up for a cup of American coffee. He poured me a cup without saying a word and sat on the workbench.

The god that made Pernell used a lot of material, let it solidify and emptied the cupboard of manly ingredients, including a big ass beard. An electrician by trade, Pernell showed up in the late afternoon, unless he worked overtime at his day job, and then he'd work until ten or eleven at night. He did not wear a wedding ring. Most workmen don't. One night he told me that he was a direct descendant of Ulysses S. Grant, and damned if he didn't look like the man.

"Robert," Pernell said, and he mumbled it as if the words had a difficult time filtering their way through that thick Brillo Pad. "Tell me this. I come in Tuesday night and left one of my sandwiches in the icebox. When I come in last night it was gone and I was planning on eatin' that sandwich. Did your old man clean out the fridge?" He spoke out of the side of his mouth, a habit he picked up chewing tobacco, I suppose.

"Not as far as I know," I said, leaning toward him to make sure I caught every word.

Pernell nodded and narrowed his eyes with one of his hands picking at the rubbery glue that stuck to the worktable.

I wasn't sure why he didn't ask my dad. He rolled the glue he'd picked off the table between his thumb and index finger and absentmindedly flicked it to the floor. We turned our heads at once to watch a few Ybor City chickens peck at bugs in a patch of grass outside the garage door.

Pernell buried his index finger deep into his beard to attack an itch and said, "So someone ate it. Stole my sandwich." He looked at me squarely, with the expression of a Civil War soldier ready to fight.

I nodded and sipped my coffee. It was good, for American coffee. Black with no sugar. I worried what he would ask next. I didn't want to lie. We got along and I think he respected me. I didn't think it would be such a big deal, the sandwich.

"Who was here on Wednesday?" he said, determined to find an answer.

"Diego, Juan, Del," I said, as Del walked in from the paint room and looked at us as if he knew we were talking about him. Del was a lanky, amiable stoner with wavy blond hair. He and Pernell got along, though they had about as much in common as two drunks who happen to stumble into the same bar. Pernell asked Del straight up if he'd eaten the sandwich, and when Del said no, Pernell nodded, told me to help myself to more coffee and he packed up his lunchbox, all except for the remaining sandwich, wrapped in tinfoil. I filled my cup and watched him walk across the shop floor to our squat little Westinghouse refrigerator where he tucked the sandwich away.

Del gave me a two-fingered salute and walked to the front of the shop rubbing white paint off his hands. He stopped to speak to my dad, who nodded and went into the office and emerged holding a few bills. Everyone got paid in cash, because the old man didn't trust Garibaldi, meaning anyone from the IRS. Del patted my dad on the shoulder and walked out. I felt like I'd just watched a touching scene from some sappy, bullshit movie of the week, though I hardly knew Del or where he went at night except that he had an on-and-off girlfriend named Eula with the kind of body that other men wanted to memorize. I'd seen her once, talking to my dad and Del in front of the shop and couldn't stop looking. She wore a white V-neck T-shirt and had the confidence of a stripper, along with high heels and hair down to her ass.

"How about your buddy, the smart dude?" Pernell said, returning from the refrigerator. "Mike something." He wasn't going to let this go.

I shook my head. Mike Harper filled in when he was desperate for money, or wanted to buy pot from Del. I played dumb as far as that was concerned, since my dad owned the shop. Mike had soft hands. He wasn't cut out for the work.

Pernell spread plans over top of the table saw and began calculating cuts. After a while, more of the nightshift guys came in. I looked up from the drawers to see my dad coming back to work in his khaki colored Dickies and a dingy white undershirt stretched to the limit. He neared my table and slipped on sawdust, which was slick on the polished concrete floor. He turned his body and caught himself and his agility surprised me.

"*Puttana*," he cursed and looked at me, as if this were my doing. "Roberto, sweep this place and throw out the trash and straighten out the tools." He wasn't mad at me. Just mad. There were too many outstretched hands he couldn't fill and a job that didn't seem to have an end. Like Del, everyone would get just enough to create resentment. And we weren't the only ones. I'd walked in his office earlier and saw him thumbing through a pile of delinquent bills. There were good years, some real good years, but this wasn't one of them.

I grabbed the broom and looked around and all I saw were boxes; boxes, with doors and drawers and shelves. These were going to be desks for a law office. They would get covered in a laminate called dappled elm, and as much as it tried to look like the real thing, it didn't. It was just another lie and I felt drained by it all. By the four dollars in my pocket, my empty gas tank, the note from my landlord hinting that rent was due, the girl in Calc-1 who I couldn't ask out for lack of funds, and the weight of it all tipped the balance on a visceral scale.

The evening drama played out in varying decibels with the table saw screaming through 120 carbide teeth. The intermittent pounding of hammers and rubber mallets emitting a cadence reminiscent of railroad workers driving spikes. The compressor purring steadily like an outboard motor. Staple guns popping. Glue pots hissing. The radio blaring out rock 'n' roll oldies. Someone cursing the router with the short in its cord. And everyone complaining about the day guys, and the misplacement of tools and disagreeing about how things should be done, or laughing about something that happened, like me replacing the toilet paper in the bathroom with sandpaper when my dad had to take a crap, and me saying that it was two hundred and twenty grit for a smooth finish. (Which he took in good humor, by the way, knowing that if the guys were laughing, they weren't thinking about money.) Then one by one, late into the night, the place would clear out and my dad would remain in his church alone.

Diego Perez jabbered like a parrot on speed while I tried to focus on the task at hand; attaching the back to a desk we were building. No one in the shop wanted to work with Diego, mainly because he fertilized the air nonstop with his bullshit and made costly mistakes, but we put up with him because we had to. My dad made sure of that. Dad collected people and gave too many second chances.

The joke around the shop was that if you asked Diego the time you'd better check with someone else because he was probably lying. This started back in June. We'd sent out for lunch and were collecting money. Diego said he was broke and the guys covered for him. The convection of heat from the unforgiving sun on our tin roof turned the shop into an oven, and that afternoon when an ice-cream truck rolled into our parking lot, we all walked out to get something cold. Diego was first in line and pulled out a ten. When Del called him a fucking liar, Diego blinked and twitched and turned away like a scolded dog that had peed in the house or chewed your shoe, and he said, "I forgot I had money." After that, it didn't matter what Diego said. When he showed up late for work, whatever delayed him was a lie. When he had to leave early for any reason, that was a lie. When he made mistakes on cabinets, which he often did, it was always someone else's fault, and that was a lie. If you called him on it, he'd make an excuse, walk outside and suck on a Marlboro, gesticulating like an epileptic. So, naturally, when Pernell's first sandwich disappeared, Diego became the prime suspect. The silent rift between them built over a couple of weeks with more sandwiches disappearing, and I enjoyed it, though I felt a little like Iago, the master manipulator.

"You're a long-distance runner, right?" Diego said so close to me I could feel the heat of his fart breath in my face.

"Diego, hold the back of the unit so we can square it," I said.

I shot the staples in, wiped away the excess glue with a damp cloth, and said I was a runner, and somehow that pulled his string.

"I was a sprinter," he said. "My high school coach said I had Olympic-caliber speed and if I stuck with it I could get a college scholarship, and likely would have gone to Florida, not Florida State because I've got this thing about maroon. When I was in the army I was the fastest guy in basic, then I twisted my knee on the obstacle course and that ruined my chances at special forces. I was going to be a sniper."

"A sniper?" I said, but the way I said it, I might as well have said bullshit.

"I was a crack shot in the Army," Diego said. "Got a dime necklace for grouping my shots within the space of a dime from 50 yards."

To understand how ridiculous this was, you'd have to know that Diego was a little over five-feet tall, weighed about 125-pounds and had the attention span of a ferret. I couldn't imagine any military force in the world giving him a gun. My dad wouldn't let him behind the saw. We'd made that mistake with another dude like him and ended up crawling around in the sawdust looking for fingers.

Pernell walked in with his lunchbox and coffee. I was happy to see him.

"How's it going, boys?" Pernell said. He turned his head and spit tobacco juice on the floor and kicked sawdust over it with his steel-toed boots.

"Peachy," Diego said, then he laughed as if he were the originator of some brilliant comedic retort.

"Diego, I left sandwiches in the fridge three nights running," Pernell said. "Next day, they were gone. Are you eating my sandwiches?"

"No, I wouldn't do that." Diego blinked and turned, pretending to focus on the desk. "I respect people's property," he said to the floor. "I learned that in the army. You can't bunk with thirty dudes without respecting their property. That's a good way to get your ass kicked."

There must have been a smirk on my face. Diego's mistakes and his bullshit contributed to jobs not getting out on time and none of us getting paid. For me, that was the crux of it, especially since I was broke, and had my sights on Cheryl, the girl in my calculus class. If I didn't ask her out before summer session ended, I could forget about it. I needed something, anything, even the smallest victory.

Diego shot one last staple in the unit and missed the mark. The staple shot through the back and blew a large chunk of mica out of the inside.

"Goddammit," I said, knowing this was another delay, another sheet of mica and a cabinet that would have to get rebuilt.

"Damn floor is slippery," Diego said looking inside of the damaged unit.

Pernell nodded without expression. "It's no good now. Take it apart."

Diego stood abruptly, checked his watch, and wiped his nose on his sleeve. "Sorry to leave you hanging, Robert, but I've got to go. Margarita's got an eye appointment and you can't drive after they dilate. We're down to one vehicle so I've got to take her." He grabbed the compressor hose and used the air nozzle to blow himself off creating a dust storm that both Pernell and I backed away from.

Pernell made it a point to tell Diego that he was taking a few days to drive his family to the Smokey Mountains. Diego said something like, "Enjoy," and walked out.

I hammered the unit apart with a rubber mallet, before the glue dried, to salvage some of the pieces, then sat on the workbench with Pernell. He poured two coffees and I watched him eat his sandwich.

Pernell finished his first sandwich, pulled out the second and opened it up on the work table. Sweet ham and Swiss with mayo on white bread. It made my mouth water. He went to the pressurized glue pot, filled with a pungent red glue called Hybond-80. It's what we used to glue the mica to the wood. It was the kind of glue that made your eyes and lungs burn. It's why the shop had two, double-wide garage doors at either end and two three-foot fans mounted into the walls turning the shop into a wind tunnel that perpetually whipped sawdust into the air creating a wood scented cloud. Pernell grabbed the gun and sprayed it in the air once to clear the line, then coated both sides of the sandwich with glue. He wrapped the sandwich in aluminum foil and tucked it in the refrigerator where he always did.

Pernell looked squarely at me. "Don't fuck with a man's food."

The next afternoon, two TECO trucks rolled to a stop in front of the shop. I walked out to speak to them with all the guys watching. Dad wasn't there, and in his absence, the shop was my responsibility. A lineman in a yellow hardhat said they were there to cut the power, but if we paid the bill downtown he'd try to put us first on his route in the morning. The lights went out and the guys stood lost, holding drills or sanders or whatever tool they had and the shop went quiet. I told the guys to break for lunch while I tracked down my dad who at that moment was at the bank trying to secure a line of credit to keep us rolling. When I spoke to him, he said he'd pay the bill that afternoon and to keep the guys working.

"How?" I asked.

"Figure it out," he said. "Everything can be done by hand except the cutting. You know that. Keep everybody working as long as there's daylight."

I sat in his chair in the cramped little office, which smelled of pine and Cuban cigars. His trust in me felt good, but looking around, the office felt like a prison.

Through the office walls I could hear Diego polluting the atmosphere and pitching it high like air being squeezed from an excited balloon. I walked out to share the news. Fausto and Juan were eating Cuban sandwiches — a sandwich they'd never heard of until they got to Tampa. Del, who had been using the big sander to sharpen hedge trimmers for some yard work, was now using a file and going at it by hand. Diego held court with Juan, Fausto and Crazy Jimmy, who ran a one-man shop in Dade City about an hour north of Tampa, but called my dad when business was slow. Crazy Jimmy talked to himself a lot and in an odd way, hence the nickname.

Diego hadn't even taken a bite of his lunch. He waved his sandwich in the air with one hand and said something about having gone to school in the service to be a codebreaker because he was bilingual and how they had him spying on Cuba. He said this twice, once in English and once in Spanish because Fausto spoke very little English. Diego took a bite of his sandwich, continued talking with his mouth full and then projectile vomited all over the cabinets we were building, and after that continued dry heaving until he doubled over on the ground writhing in the sawdust with his knees held to his chest like a baby. He had vomit and sawdust stuck to his face. Until that moment, I had forgotten about the sandwich. I felt bad for him. He was in bad shape, but I couldn't believe my luck.

Crazy Jimmy had a weak stomach. He walked outside to get some air and put his hands on his knees. I helped Diego to the bathroom. He was all hunched over and kept saying thank you to me and I said shut up, and not to worry about it. He took that as an act of compassion or a male bonding thing, like I was helping him off a battlefield.

I dumped sawdust on the vomit and shoveled it out of the shop and we cleaned food chunks out of the cabinets with mineral spirits. My dad missed the episode, but I told him about it so he wouldn't hear it from the guys.

"Well," Dad said, "he learned his lesson."

He cut everyone early and power was restored the following afternoon.

Diego took off the next two days claiming he had a stomachache, which delayed completion of the job even further. The guys in the shop were pissed because they'd only received partial paychecks, so they were all moping around like caged lions. My dad kept everyone going by promising cash bonuses when we delivered.

The longer we went without getting paid the more pissed I got. One of the dovetail drawers wouldn't square, so I yanked it out of the desk and smashed it with a hammer until it was a pile of rubble. The guys looked at me wide-eyed, but nobody said a word. In my blind stupidity, I sliced my finger on an edge of mica and it dripped blood on the floor. Del walked over and handed me a roll of masking tape to wrap it up.

"Was it worth it?" he said, smirking.

I didn't answer. Took me an hour to rebuild the drawer and I fantasized about Cheryl the whole goddamned time. She lived on campus and was into the Greek scene, and not that it's a bad thing, but she seemed like a trust fund baby. In the back of my mind, I imagined her laughing when I asked her out. I probably looked like workers who did the lawn maintenance at her parents' summer home. I wanted that victory. I needed that victory.

The night before we delivered the job, seven of us worked until two in the morning putting the finishing touches on the units. Not a word was said between Pernell and Diego, though Diego griped to me privately that he could have died. I shared the story with Pernell and he smiled with his tired eyes.

We rented two U-Haul box trucks for the delivery and loading them took some time. My dad purposely took Diego aside to make sure he'd show up.

"Johnny, I promise you. It's guaranteed. Don't even worry about it." Diego held up a Boy Scout sign and said, "Trustworthy is my middle name."

Pernell and Juan worked together prepping the units for delivery, covering corners with cardboard and wrapping them in plastic wrap. They worked in silence. Mike Harper was going on about these two girls he wanted me to meet while we carried a desk out of the shop to Del and Fausto who were waiting for us in one of the box-trucks.

"They're wild, Robert," Mike said. "They invited me over to their apartment on Saturday and said to bring a friend. It's going to be an event."

"I don't know," I said. "I might have a date."

"With a girl?" he said.

"Fuck you," I said.

Mike was a math whiz and I asked him to help me with calculus. I'd gotten Cs on my last two tests.

Space Oddity, played on the radio and I could hear Del trying to explain Ziggy Stardust to Fausto.

"*Sí, entiendo*," Fausto said. "A person."

"No," Del said. "Not a person, a persona. A character playing a part."

Five hours later we were all back, except Diego, and Pernell, who was at his day job. My dad had café con leche and Cuban toast for all of us. While we ate, he went in the office to call Diego, but couldn't get a hold of him. Diego never showed. On the way to the job we sat in dead-stop traffic for 45-minutes; the two U-Hauls full of equipment and our work van that carried the tools and hardware.

I rode in a U-Haul with Fausto, a tall Cuban with dark skin and a hint of Asian in his family tree. He'd come over on the Mariel boatlift about eight years earlier. Fausto was twenty years older than me but had not aged well, and because of ill-fitting dentures he always looked like he was smiling. He ranted about Castro being the greatest liar in history and spit shot from his dentures leaving dark spots on the gray plastic steering wheel.

Traffic crawled and I looked out my window at a guy and girl in a red Corvette convertible. He looked like one of the Hardy Boys, with perfect teeth and the kind of styled hair you can't get from a barber. The girl laughed at something he said and adjusted her blond ponytail through the back of a USF ball cap. She wore a white bikini top and I couldn't take my eyes off them, and I wanted to be in that car, in that conversation on the way to the beach with a pretty girl, making her laugh. It made me happy to watch them. She looked up at the U-Haul and caught me staring and I turned away and saw my reflection in the side view mirror; my unruly black hair, unshaven face and olive skin and I wondered what she thought of me when she saw me or if she simply looked right through me. The lane we were in slowed to a stop and the Corvette cruised away.

We didn't finish the installation, nor did we get paid. One of the credenzas got damaged jostling in the U-Haul and we had to bring it back.

Del quit on Saturday. Told my Dad that he was going to open a little shop of his own out of his father's garage and to send him his money when we got paid. He came back three weeks later to ask for his job back. He had a patch over one eye where he'd been punched in the face. He lost his vision in that eye.

After Del left, I went in the office to see my dad. His back faced the door and he was hurting a calculator when I walked in, but somehow, knew it was me.

"Roberto, get an inventory of materials and supplies and let me know what we need to fix that credenza." He looked at me with his tired face and with sawdust clinging to every part of him. A descendent of the Sicilians who came here to roll cigars, this single-minded, bull of a man moved forward always with a one-word mantra; work, work, work.

I said I would and looked around the office. The place was a hoarder's dream with wood and hardware samples leaning against every wall in no recognizable order, stacks of woodworking magazines and catalogues and a half dozen worn, low-top work boots scattered under his desk. A fine layer of sawdust covered everything, including the family pictures on the walls. Classical music played softly on a clock radio that could not be seen for the clipboards and blueprints that littered the desktop.

I made the mistake of asking for money. He turned red and bit his tongue. Literally. When the man got mad he'd stick his tongue between his teeth and bite. If he drew blood you were fucked.

"What the hell do you think is going on here?" he said. "I've got nothing. The loan is just enough to keep us going." He cursed in Italian and slammed his hand on the desk. I didn't give up. He often treated my pay like an allowance that could be withheld when necessary. My rent was late. My car running on fumes. I wanted to quit but couldn't do it. He gave me forty-dollars cash and said my rent would have to wait. Someone knocked on the door. It was Diego. I didn't say a word to him. I just eyed his funeral face and walked out.

When the guys discovered that that little *sta minga* had arrived, they gathered near the office to hear the fireworks. The office walls were made of paneling and two-by-fours without sheetrock or insulation, so we could hear every word. This was the most excitement the shop had seen since Diego spewed his guts. This was the good-riddance moment I'd been waiting for.

"Johnny," he said. "I'm really sorry that I let you down, but, I had to shoot my dog, right in front of my kids. It was horrible. I was about to leave to come here, my kids said the dog was missing, so I walked out and heard two dogs going at it in the neighbor's yard. It was still dark. They were snarling and yelping. My dog had gone rabid. He was foaming at the mouth and had attacked my neighbor's poodle, then he slunk away all hunched over and snarling. I ran back inside and grabbed my gun. The school bus stop is at the corner. God forbid the dog attacked one of the kids. I ran after the dog with my pistol and cornered him under a house. The neighbors called the cops and everything. I crawled under the house with a flashlight and felt the dog was going to come after me, so I unloaded on him with my .357. Johnny, it was terrible."

The office got quiet and I could hear the floor creaking and I imagined Diego pacing the floor with my dad sitting at his desk, looking up at him with his arms crossed, probably biting his tongue and hopefully drawing blood. The guys hung in the air like ghosts waiting for an outcome. Juan quietly translated for Fausto, who kept repeating, "*No me diga. No me diga.*"

"I had to drag the dead dog out by the leg," Diego continued. "By the time I crawled out from under the house, the cops were there with their guns on me. I put my hands up and they arrested me for discharging my weapon. My kids were crying. Margarita was hysterical. They had me in custody all goddamned day. They finally let me go when my neighbors, whose dog was killed, came and spoke on my behalf. You know what they said? They told the cops I was a hero."

The office fell silent and we went back to our work stations. Diego walked out of the office saying, "Thank you, Johnny. Thank you for understanding." He walked back into the work area without making eye contact with any of us and went to work pulling apart the damaged credenza.

That afternoon, Margarita drove up in Diego's F150, with a large breed black dog, a mix of shepherd and hound, running loose in the back of the truck. Margarita pulled up in front of the open garage door. Someone said, nice dog, and Diego went crazy and slammed his hand on the hood of the truck.

"You stupid, bitch," Diego shouted at his wife. "I told you not to bring that dog."

Diego punched the dog, hit his wife in the mouth, shoved her over to the passenger side of the truck and took off, leaving a trail of burned rubber on our parking lot. Through the back window of the truck we could see Margarita beating the shit out of Diego with her fists and we all agreed that he took the worst of it and deserved it. The bizarreness of the assault silenced us. I looked over at my old man, he was biting his tongue.

Diego was a dumbass. We didn't know what kind of dog he had or if he had two dogs.

I got a B on my next Calc-1 exam and when the professor handed my test back, I made sure Cheryl saw it. She smiled at me with her Hollywood teeth and I got this stupid gush of warmth, like a puppy having his belly scratched. I had cash from the job and I felt like a man with confidence in my pocket so I went for it.

"I have a boyfriend." She giggled and flipped her blonde hair back. "He's a Pike, so," she said, assuming I could fill in the rest. Then she turned and walked away as if she'd just told me to make sure to trim the hedges and sweep the walk when I'm done.

That afternoon I arrived at the shop in a shitty mood and kept to myself until Pernell showed. We sat on one of the work benches and drank coffee.

We were the only two in the shop. The place was still and churchlike. The big fans were off and the air was so still hardly a spec of sawdust could be seen in the afternoon sunlight. I could hear my dad on the phone in the office chasing money.

"Ya hungry?" Pernell said, pulling an extra sandwich out of his lunchbox.

"Thanks," I said, taking the sandwich. "I love these."

Pernell watched me tear into the sandwich and he smiled with a curious look, as if he knew I were swallowing a lie.

COMETS

Del Murphy awoke in room so dark it made his eyes hurt. He lay on a futon that smelled of stale sweat, in a strange house and he stared into that black hole, his mind burning through money he didn't yet have in a life that lay beyond the day. The house belonged to a biker named Butch, who at one time dated Del's wild sister May. Del was there babysitting seven garbage bags of wild growing pot that he'd harvested and was waiting for the deal to go down. He'd never had more than a dime bag in his possession, so when he lucked into that much weed, he had few options. The pot grew on some orange groves outside of Tampa and the farmer wanted nothing to do with it. He let Del have it for a share of the profits.

Del and Butch were not friends, nor had they ever been, but Butch had a place to stash the stuff and he was the only one Del knew who could sell it all. Butch wore thick, steel rings on the fingers of his right hand and had once used them to make ground meat of a man's face and skull in a bar fight, and though this knowledge left Del leery, he was determined to see the deal through.

The cell phone briefly illuminated the dingy room. It was Eula. Del ignored the call. He lifted the blackout shade letting golden light fill the room. There was something hopeful about mornings and he liked being up early. He just didn't like getting up early. The crank to the jalousie window was rusted and it took some effort to let in a little fresh air. His right hand was sore. Too many hours gripping power tools. Del grabbed a crumpled pack of cigarettes and lit one. The cell phone lit up again. It was his old man calling to warn him that Eula was looking for him and she was spitting venom. He wished his old man hadn't opened his mouth. Del had walked out on Eula and the boys again about three weeks before, and she wanted the money he'd promised her.

The room had a dank pungency to it, but even through the foul residue of sweat, body odors and other remnants of a biker whorehouse, Del smelled money. Enough to get him right with Eula, get him the hell out of his old man's house and maybe buy a used pickup. Something he could use to deliver cabinets. Nothing fancy. Even in his imaginings, it had a rusted fender. His old man already said to use the garage as a shop. That

would work fine, he just didn't want to live there.
Too many rules. His old man had gone down a
couple times for small stuff and he knew what it
was and didn't want Del tracing his footsteps.

Three hard knocks at the front door echoed
through the house and Del stiffened. Cops were
always busting this place for prostitution or drugs.
Del stared at the .38 on the nightstand. Butch left
the gun with instructions to shoot anyone who
comes in the goddamned house.

"Del, I know you're in there," Eula said in a
twang that revealed her as a transplant to Florida
from up in the South. Her voice muffled by the
front door.

"Shit," Del said quietly. "Alright. Gimme a
minute." Del's voice echoed through the house. He
dropped his feet to the cool terrazzo where he
could feel sand and stickiness from an origin that
he didn't want to contemplate. He looked at the
other three futon couches crowded into the small
room, each with stuffing bulging from worn seams
like cotton aneurisms and he wondered about the
business conducted here. He stuffed the gun in the
drawer and looked at a framed painting of a sad
clown that hung on the wall. It looked to be one of
those paint by number art projects and seemed
oddly out of place.

A series of muffled pops came from Del's body as he stretched his sinewy frame, with the cigarette hanging in his lips and smoke rising in coils. Two nights previous he'd worked until two in the morning loading cabinets at his former job and then spent the next day installing. Work for which he had not been paid and the reason he quit. He wasn't mad at Johnny or Robert about that. Del understood the cabinet business and thought maybe once he got his own shop running they'd sub work to him.

"Come on, Del," Eula said, pounding on the door. "I got the boys in the car." Eula leaned against the door frame with a long cigarette in her hand. She wore skinny jeans with slits in the knees and thighs, her long, mousey hair pulled into a ponytail.

Del stood in front of the blue toilet, shirtless, in his gray boxers, white chested with sunburned forearms. The commode had no lid or seat and the inside was stained with black mold and rust. The only sound in the house was that of toilet water running in the fill tank and Interstate traffic traveling close enough to cast moving shadows through patches of dried weeds and gray sand that passed for a front yard. Del pissed and smoked while alternately looking at the bloated vanity door that leaned against the wall and the collapsed remnants of a dead rat that lay beneath the rusted plumbing in the cabinet.

He made his way to the front door thinking of the last words his mother said to him before she ran off with that Cuban lawyer from Miami. She leaned over and kissed him on the forehead and said, "Life is too goddamned short to be unhappy." She glared at his old man, kissed May and disappeared from their lives.

Del opened the front door as far as the security chain would allow and squinted through a blast of sunlight at Eula's backlit figure. Her ten-year-old minivan burned oil on the gravel driveway. The shadows of cars flowed steadily across the gray sand yard like the workings of some giant piece of machinery.

"Goddammit Del, I'm in a hurry," Eula said trying to see into the darkness. "What're you hiding in there anyway?"

They'd had an on-and-off relationship for the better part of ten years and Del still couldn't figure out where they were going. They'd never talked about love or said the words. When they first moved in together, she brought up marriage and he said, "What's the difference between this and that?" And that's where it stayed.

Del unlatched the chain, stepped out of the house in nothing but his boxers and ran a hand through his tussled blonde hair. When they first met, Eula said he looked like that blond dude from *Hall & Oates*, and though Del took the compliment for what it was, he'd always hated that fucking band. He looked Eula up and down. She was agitated and shifting her weight from side-to-side, but had makeup on and smelled nice, sweet like magnolias. Eula's face was plain as cabbage and somewhat forgettable, but she was built like a stripper, all tits and ass and that picture was as indelible.

"Del, what are you doing here?" Eula asked, gesturing to the house. "Butch scares the hell out of me."

"He's off doing biker shit, so don't worry about it." Del mindlessly picked at flaking paint on the doorframe.

"You promised money for the boys." She shook her cigarette at him, and he stared at the red lipstick that stained the filter. "And you won't pick up my goddamn calls."

"Hell Eula, only one of em's mine." Del waved to the boys who were jumping up and down in their booster seats shouting, Daddy. One was a redhead with freckles and the other had dark skin and kinky hair.

Her face dropped and she lowered her voice. "If I was a man I would punch you right in your face. Those boys love you and you abandoned them. I need these boys in daycare. I'm a week late at Kiddie Castle and I gotta give Mrs. Mona something. I will report you this time. Don't test me."

Del looked past Eula at the boys. Delbert was his. That she lumped Carl in the deal was okay too. He liked being a sometimes dad. Del said he had fifty-bucks and disappeared back into the house to get it while Eula waited on the porch to keep an eye on the boys. Del came back wearing a gray T-shirt and faded work jeans. He produced two twenties, a five, and two ones, which he counted into Eula's extended hand like a store clerk, explaining that the cops were out, and he stopped to buy mints on the drive over. She stared at the money and asked for the twenty he kept in the side pocket of his wallet.

"It's all the cash I got," Del said.

"Goddammit, Del," she said.

Del produced the Jackson and asked if she was maybe thinking about going back to dancing. The money was good, and she always had cash back then.

"What world are you livin' in, Del?" Eula said. "Bobby's clientele don't care to see a dancer who's thirty-two and had a C-section. I'll keep waiting tables 'til I get out of school." Eula was a fast talker and she spit the words out like one of those auctioneers selling livestock.

"I quit the cabinet shop," he said out of nowhere, thinking that she might take something from that.

"That's just brilliant." She turned around clutching the money and cursed words that Del couldn't hear, then shook her head and turned back to him with that stunned expression of a person whose house has been robbed.

"Look it," Del said. "I'm working something big with Butch. After that, I'm going to open my own shop and work out of my old man's garage. He's got that detached garage out on his property. It'll make a sweet little shop."

Eula's eyes widened a bit and her face relaxed and for a moment, Del thought that she could see his dream as vividly as he could. She said, "I gotta say, that's a good idea, but it doesn't help me out and it sure as hell doesn't get you out of your responsibilities. I didn't even have goddamned milk for the boys this morning." Her voice cracked and she turned as if to walk away, then turned back around. "Goddammit, I spent the last of what I had on tuition."

She blurted this out in the way of a confession it seemed to Del. Eula was close to getting her hygienist certificate and needed him to help pay for that. Her eyes welled as she ran out of fight. She leaned in and wrapped her arms around him. Eula wasn't one to give hugs, but she took them when she needed to. Del put an arm around her and flicked the nub of his cigarette into the yard. She felt nice in his arms. The soft parts of her body felt good. Suddenly three weeks away seemed like a long time. Del watched curiously as Carl rolled down a window in the minivan and stuck his head out.

"Delbert's gotta go potty."

"Right now?" Eula pushed away from Del and checked the time on her phone.

"He's holding his pee pee."

"Eula, this house ain't kid friendly," Del said. "He can go in the yard."

"Not in sight of the whole goddamned freeway," Eula said. "Now open the door your son has to pee." Eula hustled down the porch steps, shut off the Town & Country and unbuckled the boys from their boosters. Delbert, the redhead, was four and Carl, the result of Del having previously walked out on Eula, was five. The boys ran toward the house as Del's brain worked hard on a lie. Initially, he'd flirted with the idea of showing Eula the pot just to see her expression. To prove something. That was before he knew the boys were there. The boys grabbed Del around the legs shouting, "Daddy."

"Good morning, Carl. Morning Delbert. I miss you boys." Del rubbed the boys on their heads and squeezed them. They looked cute as hell in their plaid shorts, T-shirts, and Converse All-Stars and they barraged him with questions.

"Is this your house?"

"The paint is peeling."

"Are we going to move here?"

"I like our old house better."

Del explained that he was watching the house for a friend and braced himself, swinging open the door. "Make it quick. Straight down the hall. First door on the right." The boys stepped in and became two statues gawking at the mysterious spectacle.

In the living room, there sat two sawhorses on which rested a 4 x 8 sheet of plywood. Mounded high atop the plywood was a bright green mound of marijuana that nearly reached the ceiling.

"What is it?" Carl asked, while Delbert ran to the bathroom.

Eula stood in that doorway and her lips parted. Her expression of disgust conveyed more than any string of expletives. Del shrugged with a hangdog look.

"Go with your brother right now," Eula said to Carl.

"But," the boy stammered, "what is it?"

"It's oregano," Del said. "You put it on pizza."

"Are you a farmer?"

"Go on now," Eula admonished the boy, who ran into the bathroom.

"Delbert, our daddy's a farmer," Carl announced. The sound of pee hitting water echoed through the house.

Eula stared at the mound of pot with her arms crossed and her lips clenched and her head shaking side-to-side. "How much is there?"

"Seven garbage bags or so. Maybe twelve kilos."

"Well that is about the biggest pile of stupid I have ever seen in my life. You are in way over your head. You're a cabinetmaker. You don't know a damned thing about being a drug dealer."

"Well, that just makes it sound a whole lot worse than it is."

Eula said she was getting the boys the hell out of there and that Del should do the same and walk away from this. "It's a black cloud," she said.

There was no use explaining. Eula was beyond reason. "Eula, it's a one-timer, to get on my feet," Del said, as she collected the boys. "I'm just babysitting it 'til Butch gets here with my money, then I'm out clean."

Eula marched Carl and Delbert out and upon her departure sucked the air from the room, leaving Del staring at his pile of pot. He walked out to the porch and watched Eula buckle the boys in their booster seats and then climb in the minivan. He was happy they were leaving. Butch and the Renegades were a nasty bunch. Eula turned the key, but the ignition made that clicking sound that signaled immobility and bad luck, and her body deflated into the steering wheel.

"Damn," Del said softly, seeing the idea of his day take a hard left. He walked out to the minivan and looked in the window at Eula, who seemed on the verge of a breakdown. He said he'd drive her up to Kiddie Castle and pay Mrs. Mona with his credit card and then drop her off at work and she smiled at him in a crazy, giddy way like everything in her world had been taken away from her and then given right back.

"Old MacDonald had a farm e-i-e-i-o." The boys sang and bounced up and down in their booster seats while Del drove. "And on that farm, he had some . . ."

"Oregano!" Carl sang out.

"That's enough singing, boys," Eula said.

Del's Chrysler K-car, a sun-faded blue with one shiny red door, limped along with the windows open, while the burgeoning heat of the day swirled through the vehicle like a warm hurricane carrying with it bits of ash and smoke from their cigarettes. In the back seat the boys fanned the flying ash away from their faces. They had not been on the road more than two minutes when Eula started in with the right-lane-left-lane thing. Del liked the right lane. He was never really in a hurry. Eula argued that too many cars turn in the right lane so you're always having to stop and that was frustrating.

"Would you stop telling me how to drive?" Del finally said, thinking of all those little things Eula did that drove him away in the first place. "You find the most insignificant things to control."

"I can't control anything," she said. "Not one goddamned thing in my life."

Kiddie Castle was a freestanding, rectangular block structure with the façade of a medieval castle depicted on the front. A handsome blond prince rested on one knee and gazed up at a beautiful princess who looked down on him from the tower window. Lurking behind the tower, a green dragon breathed fire into the air. Del studied the illustration as he and Eula walked the boys inside. He paid the bill and let Eula keep the cash he'd given her. On the way out, Eula held Del's arm as he escorted her through the illustrated drawbridge. When they were on the road to Alibi's, the place where Eula worked, Del told her to look in the brown grocery bag that sat between them. While Del was in the house staring at the pot, he had an idea. The way he figured it, all that pot was his. No one really knew exactly how much was there. The only one who'd seen the pile was Butch and he wouldn't know the difference. So, he stuffed a few handfuls of fat, green buds into the bag thinking that some of Eula's clients might want to buy some.

"Did you wake up and take a stupid pill?" Eula shouted. "I am not selling drugs. I am going be a hygienist." She lit a cigarette and stared out the window and they drove on in silence.

Del watched the world moving through the windshield; busy people doing busy things headed to who knows where. At an intersection, he watched a Ford F150 drive by hauling a flatbed trailer loaded with cabinets. The guys in the cab were laughing about something and Del thought, that's how dreams work. They pass before your eyes and it's up to you to catch them and make them yours. He made a mental list of things he would need besides a pickup truck, like a table saw, a compressor, power tools, wood clamps, and as the list grew he decided he'd have to write all this stuff down.

Del pulled into Alibi's parking lot and found a spot under the shade of an oak tree and the car crunched its way over the acorns that covered the black asphalt. Alibi's was a squat, white building with a flat roof, and nude Bond-girl silhouettes painted in glossy black in various dance poses all the way around. A pink neon-sign on the street corner flashed: nude girls. Inside the place was plush and attracted a mixed bag of clients, from Porsche drivers to those driving beaters as crappy as Del's. The place was located in an industrial area along with warehouses, lumber yards, and manufacturing plants and was directly in the flightpath of Tampa International. Landing planes passed so low that the sound was deafening, and it seemed as if the landing gear would skid over the roof of Del's car.

Del remembered the night he'd met Eula at a place like this. She was dancing and naked and mesmerizing. Though the girl was laid bare for all to see, soulful eyes revealed more to him than the symmetry of her veneer. She had on her ankle a scripted tattoo that read Never Again, and bruises on her arms that betrayed a bad situation. He spent all his money on her and asked her out to breakfast, and when it came time to pay, he told her that she had all his money and they laughed about that. It was the last time he saw her dance. After that it bothered him to watch. She admitted that she was living out of her car and he invited her home.

"I'll get your car fixed and pick you up later," Del said.

She reached her hand toward him and he put his leathery hand in hers. Their hands rested in front of the brown grocery bag. Del looked at Eula then and made an obvious nod toward the pot. She pulled her hand away and said, "Goddammit. I can't risk it, Del. Can't you understand that?"

"Eula, look it. If the opportunity arises, get rid of it and all the money is yours. And that's way more than what I owe you."

Eula got out of the car, leaned in the window and waited for the roar of a jet to pass. "You know, I go to hygienist school with an Indian girl named Ananya. She's a Hindu and she said, 'Karma has no menu. You get served what you deserve.'"

"Damn, Eula, you're going to give me bad luck talkin' like that."

"I'm only on a four-hour shift today, so pick me up at two o'clock and we'll get the boys," she said. Del nodded and Eula stared at the bag and frowned. "Damn it. Bobby will buy all this shit in a heartbeat and he's got the cash too." Eula grabbed the grocery bag and headed into the club and Del watched her pissed-off ass shake all the way to the door.

Del's mobile phone rang and the caller ID read Butch.

"Where the fuck are you?" Butch said. "And whose fucking car is this?"

"Man cool down," Del said. "Eula pulled in to get some dough and . . ."

"You let her in the house?"

"No. You got any jumper cables?" The line went dead. "Butch?"

When Del got to the house, Butch stood next to his chopper holding a pair of jumper cables. Butch was thick, with a ratty beard, tattoos on his arms, a pretty good-sized gut, and he wore a black leather vest with the Renegades' colors on the back. He had a gamey smell about him. Butch dropped the cables on the ground when Del pulled up. He hocked up a loogie, spit it on the hood of the minivan and said, "Get this the fuck out of my driveway." Then he walked in the house. Del pulled his car next to the minivan and got it started then asked Butch if he'd follow him to the gas station for ride back. Butch gave him the finger and continued rolling himself a joint. Del drove the minivan to a Firestone and walked three miles back to the house. Heat waves shimmered like mirages over the asphalt streets, and with every step under the pounding sun Del got closer to the house and the sickly feeling of having made a mistake. It was like being on a bad acid trip and all he could do was ride it out. By the time he arrived, sweat burned in his eyes and his jeans and T-shirt were stuck to his skin. He walked in the front door thinking about a cold Mountain Dew and stopped to let his eyes adjust to the darkness. Then the room went black.

Del wasn't out long, at least he didn't think he was. His right eye throbbed and his head felt like the worst tequila hangover he'd ever had. He sat up and spit blood on the floor from the hole he'd bitten in his tongue and the metallic taste of it made him nauseous. He looked up with his good eye to see Butch sitting in a chair with the .38 revolver in his lap. Del touched his swollen eye. It was purple and the whites were red where blood vessels had burst.

"The fuck did you do that for?" The words slurred from Del's mouth.

"The pile looks light."

"That why you hit me?"

"I hit you cause I don't like you," Butch said. "I know you fucked the deal with May. She liked it up the ass too. Hard." Then he chuckled and Del realized that was the first time he'd seen Butch's teeth. There were a couple missing, but they weren't bad teeth considering, and he thought about Eula and how she could identify which teeth those were. She would have known that one was a cuspid and the other a bicuspid or something like that.

The room teetered. Del tried to rise but felt the blood rush from his head and plopped back to the floor. Blood and saliva seeped from his open mouth like bright red syrup. He pushed himself back against the wall and focused on Butch with one good eye. Butch accused him of stealing some pot.

"Until I get paid it's my pot," Del said. "So, fuck you. How did you know anyway?" Del surveyed the pile.

"I didn't, you stupid fuck," Butch said.

Butch shifted the revolver in his lap and smoked a joint. Del looked at the gun and asked if Butch was going to shoot him and Butch said he might. Del said that would be stupid seeing how he was the only one who knew where the pot grew and when it'd be ready to harvest again. Butch rocked in his chair, pointed the gun at Del's face and cocked it. Del stared at the barrel. His stomach cramped. He got tunnel vision. He didn't want to crap his pants but felt he might.

"You pussy." Butch waved the gun. "Get the fuck out of here. When we figure this shit out you'll get your cut. Or we might just kill you and your fucking bitch in your sleep."

Del wavered and reached for one of the sawhorses to lift himself up. His legs wobbled like one of those wooden puppets held together by rubber bands. The burning pot smelled good. Blood pooled in his mouth and he spat on the floor. "That's about thirty pounds of pot. I want a third or next time I take the deal somewhere else." He went to the bedroom and grabbed his bag, then took a Mountain Dew from the fridge. Butch didn't move. He sat there with the .38 in his lap staring at the mound of pot with a shitty, half-assed smirk on his face.

Del staggered through the sandy yard like a desperate man emerging from the desert. He sat in the spinning car and with trembling hands opened the Mountain Dew. It burned in his mouth, tingled all the way to his stomach and then came right back up. He leaned out the door and vomited in the sand. The next sip was cold and stayed down, and he started the car and struggled to keep it between the lines. A mile or so up the road he pulled into a parking lot and turned off the engine.

The cell phone woke him, and he looked around with no recollection of having driven there. It was Eula, who surprisingly wasn't pissed off that he was late. Though his head ached and his eye throbbed like a heartbeat on his face, the dizziness had subsided. His vision was still fuzzy in one eye, but he could drive.

Eula waved and smiled when Del pulled up, but that all faded when she saw his face. She went back in the club and brought out ice in a baggy which she held to his purple eye, and he thought in that moment that she'd make a good dental hygienist. On the drive to get the boys Eula said she was sorry that the deal didn't work out and Del said, "It ain't over yet." Then Eula pulled out a wad of cash and beamed. Bobby had given her a thousand dollars for the pot. Del smiled and didn't let on that what he'd given her was worth twice that. She looked at him then, with discerning eyes. It was a respectful kind of look, and he could tell that she was thinking about being a regular family and that he was someone on whom she and the boys could rely. It felt good to be thought of that way in the short term. To come through on a promise and be admired. He imagined himself vested in that role. The provider. The man of the house. Working out of his own cabinet shop. Del Murphy Cabinets, he'd call it. Yet, even in that moment of imagining, which is usually as good as things get, it was too much to live up to. It wasn't in him to hold up to that kind of pressure over the long haul. Living with Eula and the boys, it always felt temporary. Like that part of his life was just a weigh-station on the way to somewhere else. Nevertheless, under her approving eyes, he felt the pendulum swing back toward her and the unhappiness that drove him to leave faded.

"Did you hear about the comet that's visible in the night sky?" she said. "One of my customers was talking all about it. He's an amateur astronomer or something like that."

"I hadn't heard anything about it," Del said.

"It's called the Hale-Bopp Comet and it won't come around again for another 2,400 years. Can you imagine that? It has been traveling that way for billions of years all around the universe."

"That's pretty cool," Del said. Though he really didn't care about it one way or the other. Eula always latched on to oddities like that.

"I'd like to see that comet," she said. "To say I did. Because if you miss it now, no one on this earth will ever see it again. Why don't you come home tonight? We'll grill burgers and hot dogs and watch the comet. And then we can say we saw it."

"I think I'd like that," Del replied.

They stopped by Kiddie Castle on the way to pick up the minivan and Eula told the boys that Daddy was coming home. The boys asked about Del's face while he was switching out the booster seats and he explained that he'd had an accident at work.

Del followed the minivan onto the interstate for the ride across town and he thought about Eula's smiling face and it made him happy. It felt good, the four of them together. Despite his pounding head and failing vision in one eye, he held tenuously to a hopeful feeling. A Tom Petty tune played on the stereo and he turned it up. As he passed by Butch's front yard, he looked down from the raised highway to see a swarm of cop cars surrounding the house, and bikers in handcuffs bent over police cruisers, and Del sunk in his seat, a stamp of that scene imprinted in his mind as the place where dreams go to die. He wondered if others driving past that scene in that moment saw what he did.

HEROES

The guys who spoke at these meetings seemed to find it cathartic. They had to say it out loud, to hear the words and to see the bobbing heads to know they weren't alone. Pernell Grant never spoke, not once in ten years. Though given his size and constitution, with his thick arms and healthy beard, his presence was certainly not ignored. Most would look at him and wonder, infantry or perhaps a gunny before time and the friction of living took their toll. No one pushed him to say anything. Lieutenant Guthrie, a gray-haired black man, a former Navy chaplain, would now and again ask if he wanted to speak and Pernell would smile with his eyes and shake his head. Pernell listened and looked at the other men feeling both thankful and guilty that he had his limbs.

The musty portable sat on the property of the VA hospital and the hollow floor suffered under Pernell's weight when he walked around. There were seven men in attendance, and they sat in a semi-circle sipping on coffee or bottles of water, and a few, like Pernell, carried the faint smell of cigarettes and alcohol.

A man named Smalley spoke of the la Drang Valley as if he had been there the previous day. Some of the men looked at their shoes as he spoke or chose a spot on the worn brown carpet. Smalley stared into that void where memories burn. He'd held his confession for more than three decades.

Smalley looked like a little old man now, thin and bald with white hair above his ears, a bulbous nose and gin blossoms that spread like tributaries. He was fair skinned with scars on his face from patches of skin cancer that had eaten away at him. Probably a golfer, Pernell thought. Seemed to be the kind of man with hobbies to occupy his mind. He'd shared idle conversation with Smalley during coffee breaks and learned that the man had spent his life as an accountant. Smalley wore a collared, long-sleeve shirt with a mechanical pencil clipped in the front pocket and black dress shoes that looked uncomfortable as hell. Looking at him now, it was hard to imagine him in the jungle with an M16 shouting, "Hoorah!"

Pernell watched Smalley struggle through the story and wondered why the passing decades erased some memories and left others, and why this story, which sat quietly burning for so long, chose this moment to breath. In some ways, all the stories were the same and ran together like a jumbled river of letters and words. It didn't make them any less true. Smalley didn't think he would last another day. No one was looking. It was a small wound, self-inflicted, but he made sure it was enough to get him home. Heads bobbed without judgment. Pernell understood better than most and thought Smalley a brave man.

Pernell thought about the day Lindy got blown to hell and he stood abruptly, nodded to the other men and walked out. A sure giveaway that he was hiding something. But weren't they all?

If Pernell were a barfly, he'd go find one to sit in, but then he'd have to justify the expense to Maria. He wondered if Johnny was at the shop. The shop was a good place to be. Pushing wood through that screaming saw, getting lost in the white noise. An activity that required total focus if you wanted to keep your fingers. Of course, Johnny wouldn't be there on a Saturday night.

Pernell had just turned 18 and was out drinking beer with his friends when the fight broke out. It ended quickly when Pernell got involved and they took him downtown. The fight was over a girl who wasn't even Pernell's girl. Just a girl fending off advances from a couple of other Tuscaloosa boys who were too drunk to fight. One of the boys ended up with a broken jaw and the other a broken nose and Pernell's hand puffed up like rising dough and throbbed. He could have been charged as an adult, but when the judge saw the size of him and heard about his family history and their time-honored service to country, he told Pernell to enlist and make his family proud.

The following day, Pernell and his father drove to the Marine Corps recruiting center in the strip mall near the Baskin & Robbins, and afterward they went to get some ice cream. His father tried to explain war over a couple of chocolate sundaes. His old man wasn't much of a talker. He said, "War's a roulette wheel and ain't nothing can be done about that." He stirred the chocolate into the vanilla until it all turned gray. "Some'll walk though without a scratch, others won't make it past day one. Them who make it out are the walkin' wounded." Then he stared into his ice cream, as if the words he sought were there and could be tasted. Pernell thought about that day eleven months later, on a night patrol under a canopied jungle, and he understood what his father couldn't say and the power he'd missed in that vacant stare.

Butterflies fluttered in Pernell's gut for the first month. A nervousness you could say, but no real fear and no real fighting. It was like camping in the woods with your buddies. You could hear the booms and see jets flying overhead and sometimes the earth would shake and there would be pops of gunfire, but the war, the actual fighting, was happening somewhere in the distance. Pernell hadn't even clicked the safety off his weapon. All the evidence pointed to a conflict, but Pernell hadn't seen it for himself, so the reality of it was merely speculation. Then one sunny afternoon, Mark Lindy, a blue-eyed boy from Mississippi, stepped on a Bouncing Betty, and lost his clothes, his legs, and his genitals. That was something, and the sight of it settled in deep.

Pernell removed his work boots on the front porch and carried them inside. Maria rolled herself toward the front door to greet him and she looked at his white socks when he walked in to make sure those boots weren't on his feet. The television played some kind of cop show and cast a bluish light into the darkened living room. Pernell walked through the room without glancing at the screen.

"Don't expect dinner to be warm," Maria said, rolling her way into the kitchen behind him.

"Don't matter," he said.

"Nothing matters, does it?" she snapped back. "You're gone from five in the morning until ten every night and now on a Saturday night, you want to go swap war stories. If you don't want to be home, what's the point?"

He couldn't blame her for wanting something better. Five years planted in that chair thanks to a drunk driver. She had conveniently lost all recollection of the accident and the events surrounding it, but Pernell had not, and it burned, perhaps in the same way that Smalley's story had for so long.

Pernell grabbed a piece of cold fried chicken from a dish on the stove. "It's good," he said as a morsel of chicken hit the floor.

"The goddamned house is clean, Pernell," Maria said and told him to sit at the kitchen table so he wouldn't drop crumbs everywhere. She rolled to the refrigerator to get the pitcher of sweet tea she'd made earlier, placed it in her lap and rolled herself to the table. He knew better than to try and help. He noticed the gray in her hair. She used to dye it but gave up on that a while back.

"I know you're in a hurry to get to work in the mornings, but can you at least put the dishes in the washer the right way. Flat dishes in the back, bowls in the front. I'm tired of having to come around behind you to fix it."

"Does it make a difference?"

"If you put bowls and plates together they don't get clean. It hurts me to lean in there."

He nodded and picked meat off a chicken bone with his front teeth, which made the hairs around his mouth shiny. She watched him and he knew she was thinking hard on something that she wanted to say, maybe a lot of things she wanted to say. He thought to when their conversations where breezy and sprinkled with laughter, with her feet rubbing on his beneath this very table.

"Macy's got homecoming next month," Maria said, abruptly. "The dress she wants is a hundred and fifty dollars. I gave her a limit of seventy-five."

Pernell worked on a piece a chicken stuck between his teeth and chose his words carefully. "She's been getting good grades," Pernell said. He knew about the dress because Macy had told him, and he'd promised her the money. He didn't have it yet, but knew he'd get it from Johnny. Money was owed.

"That girl breaks curfew every damned weekend," Maria said. "And you're going to reward her."

"Maybe if we give her a reason to make good decisions," Pernell said, then stopped when Maria abruptly turned to roll away.

Pernell looked at the half dozen prescriptions bottles on the kitchen counter and the stack of envelopes next to them. If there was something due, she'd have said so by now. Pernell worked as an electrician by day and a cabinetmaker at night. After the accident, he'd rebuilt the kitchen and lowered the countertops for Maria. Johnny had come over to help.

Maria turned back before she left the room and said, "The girl needs a car too, Pernell. You gonna run out and buy one of those? And then she'll need money for college."

"One thing at a time," Pernell said. "We'll look for something used."

"I'm going to bed," Maria said and rolled out of the room.

Maria was bitter before the chair, having lost faith in the life she thought they'd have together, and Pernell knew that. The look on her face said it all. "Is this all there is?" She'd gotten a taste of something different and it wasn't a working man's life. He'd thought of cutting out, maybe heading back up to the South. But afterward, after the accident, there was no easy way out of this battle.

Pernell poured a glass of vodka over ice, walked out to the porch and smoked an unfiltered Camel. The crickets and frogs filled the night air with their monotonous cadence and before long, his eyes felt heavy and he may have nodded out. Maria's wheelchair squeaked behind him and he turned. She wore a nightgown, and in the moonlight, he could see the dark outline of her breasts.

"Pour me one of those, would you?" she said. "I can't sleep." Pernell kept the vodka in one of the upper cabinets.

"Shouldn't have one with pain killers," Pernell said and hesitated, then walked into the kitchen and poured her one anyway. A peace offering.

Maria took it silently and they drank and listened to the business of the night, a soundtrack of sorts to their growing tension. A series of bad decisions, Pernell thought. That's how they arrived here. We all make hundreds, maybe thousands of decisions every day, like what bar to walk into on your eighteenth birthday, where to step when you're on a trail in the jungle, or what road to drive home on when you've had a few too many, and every decision you make alters your life, sometimes a little and sometimes a lot.

He felt her gaze and turned, and their eyes met. You'd have to be a pretty goddamned good liar to keep someone from reading your thoughts at that point. At once he saw in her face a mix of emotions, anger, disappointment, desire, and in that moment of vulnerability he felt a primal urge, but it quickly faded, and it was just as well. Maria had neither the desire nor the sensation to act on that impulse. On occasion though, her legs would jump or stiffen without the conscious want to do so.

"Someone at the shop had been eating my sandwiches," he began, just to break the silence. Maria looked toward him but said nothing. "Last summer, 'round the time we drove up to the Smokies." Maria nodded. "Not that I really need it." Pernell rubbed a hand on his gut, which didn't seem very big, but he could carry a lot of weight.

"Doctor say anything about that at your physical?"

Pernell shook his head. A lie of omission. Maria had her secrets and Pernell had his own. After three weeks of disappearing sandwiches, Pernell decided enough was enough and one afternoon, while he sat with Robert having coffee at the cabinet shop, he sprayed a sandwich down with glue; red, nasty, pungent stuff, wrapped it back up in tinfoil and stuck it in the refrigerator.

"Turned out to be Diego," Pernell said, "a little, nervous dude who never could figure shit out." Pernell smiled. "Diego had eaten the sandwich at lunchtime and gotten sick as hell and threw up all over the shop."

Maria made a sound in her throat, and Pernell looked at the night sky as if searching for something there. "Point is, you have to want," Pernell said. "You have to want something, anything. If you stop wanting." His voice trailed off. He looked over at Maria and she was asleep in her chair.

"When I get home . . ." Lindy said to Pernell, while they were humping through the jungle. That was as far as Lindy got before he stepped on the mine. Pernell was behind Lindy and took shrapnel in his hip and thigh. It knocked him off his feet and burned like hell but didn't hurt as bad as he thought it would. He dropped his gear, scooped up Lindy and ran with him. He was still young enough to think Lindy could be saved, even five clicks from camp.

In the darkness, Pernell ran with the burden of half a man over his shoulder but couldn't move forward. His muscles burned yet he had no traction. He gasped for air like a fish on the shoreline. The stickiness of warm blood pulsed onto his chest in slow beats, ran down his torso, flowed into his open mouth and filled his lungs until he couldn't breathe, and he drowned in it.

Pernell jolted up in bed and wondered what Lindy had wanted when he got home. He was in a flop sweat. That's what they called it in the Corps. He looked into the darkness and could hear his heartbeat in his ears. Maria would be mad as hell that the sheets were wet. Pernell rose and dressed with Maria snoring softly. No reason to be quiet about it. The pain killers and vodka would keep her out. And Macy, hell, she'd sleep until noon. Pernell heard her sneaking in a little after two, well after curfew.

It was Sunday morning. The roads were quiet this time of day and Pernell was happy when the sun finally crept over the horizon. A man's home should be his respite against the world and at one time his was. The air seemed thick there now. He couldn't even load the goddamned dishwasher right.

Pernell pulled his Toyota pickup into a Dunkin' Donuts and ordered black coffee and a jelly filled. The clerk, a young woman of about nineteen with a nose ring and red stripes in her mousy hair, seemed anxious at the sight of him, so he smiled to be less intimidating.

"When ya hit a certain age, you don't sleep anymore," he said to her.

"My mom's that way," the girl replied, placing his order on the counter. "Why does that happen?"

Pernell knew the answer but shook his head as if he didn't. How do you explain life to a teenager? Or guilt that burns in your gut? He gave the girl a five, said to keep it, then sat at a table alone and thumbed through an old newspaper that someone had discarded. One day to the next it didn't matter, all the stories seemed the same as those printed any other day of the week.

Pernell left the donut shop at eight-thirty. The shop would be open after nine. Johnny always worked a few hours on Sundays and Robert would stop by with Cuban coffee if he wasn't in one of his little snits about money or whining about how hard his life was. Pernell had to remind himself the boy was only nineteen and didn't know shit.

"General Grant." Johnny saluted when Pernell walked in the shop, which always made Pernell smile. Johnny was a squat Italian, an ex-Marine with toes missing from his time in Korea, which made him walk like a penguin. The man was always happy when he was working. "Maria must have kicked you out."

"Figured I'd get a few hours in if you need me," Pernell said, and he told Johnny about the homecoming dress and the cost and Johnny said he was happy he had boys and he handed Pernell an envelope with three hundred cash.

Johnny never turned anyone away who wanted to work. The shop was loaded up, and cabinets in various stages of completion were stacked everywhere. Johnny handed Pernell a clipboard and said that if he could cut all the drawers and doors the guys could start gluing and assembling on Monday.

The place smelled alive and Pernell felt good being there. It was a place where things were built to last. Pernell thought it funny that in Johnny's office there were photo albums loaded with pictures of cabinets and office furniture, but not one picture of the guys who worked here.

"You eat breakfast?" Johnny said. "I'll call Roberto and tell him to bring egg sandwiches on Cuban bread."

Pernell said that sounded good and he thought back to when he used to fish on Sunday mornings. It was peaceful, but Maria didn't eat fish.

Pernell weighed two hundred thirty-two pounds when he enlisted. Eight months into his tour, with one wound, a bout of malaria, and dysentery that squirted out of him like lentil soup, he was down to one hundred eighty-seven.

His tour ended on a night that Pernell found himself alone, with most of his platoon silenced or screaming amidst confusion and noise and smoke. The enemy was everywhere and nowhere running through the jungle with those AKs shooting 7.62

rounds. Airstrikes lit up the jungle and rang in his ears. The jungle has a way of spinning you around. A thought flashed about his old man and the cigar box his mother handed him after the funeral. The box was stuffed with trinkets, some old black and whites, a letter from the Corps, and buried under it all, a medal. Pernell held his position, guarding a single trail in the dense brush. He decided that one way or another it would be his last night in that goddamned war. In the morning, he limped out using his weapon as a cane, with a 5.56 round from his M16 having destroyed much of his calf. A magic bullet.

Pernell came home before going to the cabinet shop for the evening. Maria was napping and Macy's door was cracked. She was staring at a book and bobbing her head with earbuds in her ears. Pernell had bought her one of those iPods for her birthday and it was mostly filled with noise, though she did have some good country music in there. The girl was thin, like her mom and she had wavy, Cuban hair, but thankfully she'd inherited Pernell's height. Tall for a girl.

Pernell watched Macy and thought back to the night of her first sleepover. She'd just turned twelve and begged to spend the night at a girlfriend's house. A bunch of girls were having a sleepover and she'd gotten invited, which was a pretty big deal. Maria had worked late again and when Pernell dropped Macy off, he gave her a twenty, in case they went to the mall or a movie, said to have fun and to call in the morning when she wanted to get picked up. Macy gave him a hug and said, "Love you, Daddy. You're my hero." Pernell smiled at the memory. Didn't get much better than that.

"What?" Macy said, with an air of indifference seeing her dad at the door.

Pernell stepped in the door and put a finger to his lips and Macy removed the buds from beneath her curls. "Your mom's sleeping," he whispered.

"What's up?" she said.

"Got something for you," Pernell said, pulling a bank envelope out the back pocket of his jeans. "It's for the dress."

"Thanks," she said, and smiled taking the envelope without much enthusiasm. She thumbed through the bills then looked up with the expression of a lottery winner. "But mom said!"

"You get the dress you want," Pernell said.

Macy jumped off the bed and hugged him with the envelope clutched in one hand. Pernell said he wanted her to start coming home before curfew. She promised she would and, in that moment, he was sure she meant it.

"If you can keep your word, we're going to see about getting you a car."

"Oh my God! Are you kidding?"

"Something used," Pernell said.

"I'll be on time," she said and hugged him again. "I promise."

Pernell squeezed his little girl and said he was going to work at the shop. Working two jobs had its benefits. Pernell and Maria fought less, because he wasn't around to fight. He also brought in more money and the mood in the house changed significantly when there was more money to go around. He didn't see as much of Macy, but moments like this one made it worth the time away.

On the way to the shop, Pernell thought again of the night Macy had the sleepover. That's when the war began. Pernell dropped Macy off, went home, dressed in his good jeans, a checkered shirt that he ironed himself, and cowboy boots which he buffed to a military shine. He liked country-western music and had this crazy idea of surprising Maria and taking her out. They could listen to some live music and have a couple of drinks at the Dallas Bull over on 301. But Maria came home, said she didn't feel well and walked straight into the bedroom. Pernell caught a whiff of alcohol, but otherwise, she smelled nice. She'd worn perfume to work. Maria went into the bathroom, shut the door behind her, locked it and turned on the shower. Pernell sat on the bed and stared at the bathroom door, then went to a little pub called Good Time Charley's where he drank and played pool with strangers until two o'clock in the morning. When he came home that night, he pulled his boots off and slept on the couch.

Stay away. That was the message from Maria, though she never actually said the words. She wanted a confrontation. She wanted to share that burning guilt inside her, but Pernell would not give her the satisfaction. Speculating on something is one thing, but knowing for sure, that's when the real damage gets done. Better to keep this war at a distance.

The call came on Pernell's cell at 2:30 in the afternoon, while he was pulling Romex through a new build on a cold ass January day. A pick-up towing a trailer had run a stoplight. Maria's boss died at the scene. Maria was in the passenger seat of his Porsche. Her car was found two days later in the parking lot of the downtown Hilton.

Pernell didn't share the results of his physical with Maria. She just complained about his paycheck being short and wanted to know why he'd missed work. People often looked at him and thought because of his size and strength he was indestructible.

"You're headed for a train wreck," the doc at the VA said to Pernell, thumbing through the results. There was a growing blockage in one of his arteries. He gave Pernell a list of things to do, eat more fish and salads, exercise, and cut down on the coffee. Stop dipping tobacco and quit smoking. He prescribed blood thinners and medications for blood pressure and cholesterol and told Pernell he'd be wise to lose about thirty-five pounds.

After his doctor visit, Pernell pulled his truck under the shade of a live oak at a park. As he rolled to a stop, acorns crunched beneath the tires. He poured a cup of coffee from his thermos and thumbed through the prescriptions. Same thing had happened to his old man. Congestive heart failure. The man filled with fluid and couldn't breathe. He suffered. Too goddamned long. Bills piled up. He had to quit work and they lost their house. Pernell could see this happening to him and if it did, where would that leave Macy and Maria? He crumbled the prescriptions and tossed them on the floor of the truck.

The following Monday, Pernell was up as usual, at 4:30 in the morning, brewing coffee and making sandwiches. He filled his thermos and he made four sandwiches with sweet ham, Swiss cheese, and healthy slathering of mayonnaise on both slices of the bread, and he wrapped them in tinfoil. Two, he would eat on his job as an electrician. The other two he'd take to the cabinet shop to eat during the evening, or store in the shop refrigerator. He put a cast iron skillet on the stove and fried eggs with bacon and had toast with butter and honey.

After breakfast Pernell thumbed through the envelopes on the kitchen counter. He grabbed one out of the stack, wrote the check himself and put a stamp on the envelope. It was the life insurance.

Maria paid each bill on the last day it was due and Pernell didn't want this one to be late.

Pernell felt winded before he'd even walked into the meeting, like he'd taken a flight of stairs at a full sprint or carried a friend's dead body five clicks though the jungle. The feeling in his heart was carefree and he smiled at the other vets and said hello and they could tell he was in a good mood. Tonight, Pernell thought, he might share a story about how to beat death.

Before sitting with the other men, Pernell stood by the coffee with a hand in his pocket fingering the points of the star he'd pulled from his old man's shoebox, and he recalled the words on that letter, *for valor.*

About an hour into the meeting, Pernell's left arm began to hurt, more of an ache than anything else. This is how it starts, he thought. The pain radiated to his neck and he felt heartburn in his chest and cold sweat over his body. He knew what it was but didn't feel as though something was being taken away. Not like Lindy, stepping on that Bouncing Betty while talking about wanting something. It could have been anything, a hamburger, a milkshake, or a girl. Lindy never got any of those things. He died randomly on that roulette wheel. He died wanting.

In the middle of another man's confession, Pernell, out of nowhere, said, "Smalley." The man who was speaking stopped and looked over at Smalley, who looked at Pernell confused, but saw in his face a man in distress. Smalley rose and went to Pernell, who sat across the semicircle. The other men leaned forward in their seats, as if it were a moment before an action should take place. Pernell leaned toward Smalley and whispered his confession and the men were kindred.

Smalley put a hand on Pernell's thick shoulder. The war was over.

A Dog Named Hoarse

The shop was a powder keg that at any moment could explode. The sawdust floating around would ignite from the heat coming off the men and burn the place to ash. The mood of the place was palpable, like when heat becomes visible on black pavement. We'd all been working twelve to sixteen-hour days, but money had been slow to come in and that had everyone on edge. There'd already been a shouting match this morning between Del and Fausto over something stupid, like Del routing toward the table saw, which sprayed cuttings that direction and prevented sheets of wood from sliding smoothly. Fausto rattled off something in Spanish to Del. Called him a *pendejo*, among other things. Del said fuck you and kept routing. Crazy Jimmy worked in the corner alone, cursing at crooked drawer faces and talking to himself. I stared out the garage door thinking about being someplace else.

My old man showed just before noon with piles of Cuban comfort food; Cuban sandwiches, *papa rellena*, guava and cream cheese pastries, and *café con leché*. The food of Ybor City. We took a long lunch sitting on our low worktables and he told us that when we delivered the job we'd all get bonuses. We'd all heard that before and it was getting old. No one said a thing, though the food did lift spirits a bit.

It was about that time that a three-legged dog hopped into the shop like a cool breeze through the open garage door. I fed him scraps of ham and roast pork from my sandwich and Del gave him a cup of water. The dog visited with each one of us wagging his tail. The scrawny dog wore no collar and had war wounds from living on the streets. Some cuts and patches of missing hair. Dog scars.

We went back to work and the dog hung around the rest of the day, lying on the cool concrete floor and drinking water from the cup Del had put down. He came and went of his own accord and we put him out that night when we locked up.

The first day the dog hopped in, my Dad tried to shoo him away. After I fed the dog, Dad shook his head with a defeated look and said, "Goddammit. Now he's ours." And Del said, "Well, Johnny, he fits right in with this bunch." Which made us chuckle.

We called him Dog for the first week, until he barked at the feral chickens that congregated in the alley behind the shop. The bark was deep and raspy, like Dog had been choked at one time and never recovered. So, Del, I think it was Del, took to calling him Hoarse and the name stuck.

A wiry mutt, about the size of a Jack Russell, Hoarse had short, brown hair with white patches on his chest and near his front paws. He walked around with his tongue out and seemed happy, despite the missing limb. Having a three-legged dog running around the shop changed the mood of the place. Over the next couple of weeks, the guys all brought in gifts for Hoarse. Del brought two tin dog bowls. Crazy Jimmy brought in a squeaky chew toy. Fausto shared leftover steak scraps from home. One of the night guys, Sarge, brought a mat for Hoarse to use as a bed. I was in my last semester of college, on the five-year plan, so I typically showed up in the afternoons. One afternoon I arrived to see that Hoarse had an azure blue collar around his neck and dog tags. My old man had taken him to the vet and filled a five-gallon bucket with dog chow.

At Publix, I picked up a box of dog biscuits and taught Hoarse how to sit, and fetch using a scrap of pine. Smart dog, caught on quick. Or maybe he already knew these tricks.

Hoarse must have been someone's dog at one time, because the left hind leg was neatly taken. Surgically removed I would imagine. Impossible to know what that's like, unless it happened to you, having part of you abruptly gone. It didn't seem to bother Hoarse.

Dad's office had a window unit and Hoarse took to sleeping at the old man's feet. When Dad came out to the work floor, for whatever reason, Hoarse followed him like a three-legged foreman. When Dad went to the bathroom, which we'd basically framed with half-inch plywood and two-by-fours, Hoarse sat outside and waited.

Hoarse became the shop dog, but he was really my old man's dog, and following his lead, we began leaving Hoarse in the shop at night.

Every other Monday, Nate arrived in a massive box truck full of materials we'd ordered from the supply house: wood, laminate, staples, glue, and so on. Nate had been our delivery guy for about five years and we'd gotten to know him, as well as you can know a delivery guy, when you converse with him every other week for twenty minutes, or however long it took to unload. A weathered fifty-five or so, Nate had fair-skin and reddish hair, and from the time we met him, he walked with a stiff-legged limp. Sort of like a penguin. Sort of like my old man who'd lost a few toes from frostbite in Korea. I never asked Nate about it. That's not something you ask someone you don't know well. Nate was also a heavy smoker, unfiltered Camels, and he talked like a smoker. Whenever he pulled up, he'd climb down from his truck with a cigarette in his hand, take a couple of long drags and flick it into the street before he walked in. Everything in the shop was flammable.

Nate showed up the Monday after Hoarse arrived and Hoarse stiffened his front legs, lowered his head, sniffed and growled a raspy growl. Shop security. Nate scratched Hoarse on the head and the dog rolled to his back and showed his belly. We all stood there watching, waiting to unload the materials, exchanging pleasantries. Nate scratched the dog's belly and Hoarse went into spasms of hind leg shaking.

When Nate drove away, Hoarse howled like a coyote with his eyes closed and his neck extended to the sky. It was funny as hell to watch. Then he hopped back to my dad's office and scratched on the door.

Two weeks later, Nate showed again and Hoarse began running in circles and barking his raspy bark before Nate even parked the truck. When Nate walked in, Hoarse was all over him, barking, licking him, and jumping up on his one hind leg like a circus dog performing a balancing act. This time, Nate reached into his pocket and produced a dog biscuit. Hoarse snatched the biscuit and rolled over on his back. Nate smiled and watched him.

"That dog loves you," my dad said to Nate.

"That's a helluva dog you got here, Johnny," Nate said. "Sweet dog." Nate reached down and scratched Hoarse's belly and talked baby talk to him.

A few of us unloaded the materials while Dad gave Nate our next order, which Nate looked over and put on his clipboard with Hoarse standing between them. The guys went back to work and I grabbed the last of the order, two gallons of white glue.

"Listen Johnny," Nate said, scratching Hoarse on the head. "I can't make it on Monday the eleventh. Veterans day. I'm taking off. I'll be here the twelfth."

This intrigued me and I had the feeling it had something to do with his limp.

"Are you a Vet?" I asked.

Nate nodded. "I was in Nam in sixty-eight and sixty-nine. That's where I lost my leg." He pulled up his khaki workpants above his boots and showed us his prosthetic leg. The leg was that light beige skin tone that in no way resembled any skin color. "I was twenty-two and stepped on a Bouncing Betty."

"Damn Nate," my dad said. "You were deep in the shit."

I thought my dad might say something about his time in Korea, but he didn't.

"I want to show you guys something," Nate said, pulling out his wallet, with Hoarse jumping up and down wanting his attention and sniffing around his prosthetic leg. Nate showed us a wrinkled, black and white photograph of a Vietnamese family; a man and woman with two kids. The couple looked to be in their twenties and the kids were under five. "This is a guy I killed," Nate said.

Dad and I glanced at each other.

"I had orders to watch a trail and to shoot anyone who came my way. He came walking down the path, middle of the day, humming a tune. Shot him with my M16. Right here." Nate pointed to his chest. "He was the only person I shot in that war. I checked his pockets and found that picture. He was the town barber. Had a wife and kids. A regular guy until he was called to war, just like me. He had an AK-47 on him, so I had to shoot him."

Nate took the picture back, looked at it for a moment and tucked it in his wallet.

"I think about this guy on Veteran's day, you know?" Nate said. "I think about his kids and his wife. I didn't know him. Had nothing against him. Hell, any other day, he might have been cutting my hair. But that's a lot of what war is."

Dad nodded like he understood, and I nodded, like I understood.

Nate patted Hoarse on the head and shook our hands. He always shook our hands, and he walked out to his truck. I went back to hang doors on the kitchen cabinet uppers I'd been working on, and I turned to see my dad flag Nate down before he drove off. Nate rolled down the window of the cab and they spoke for a minute or so. I could see Nate shake his head, then smile broadly.

Dad picked up Hoarse and handed him to Nate through the window of the truck. Then he gave him the two tins and the bucket of dog food. Like me, the guys in the shop had stopped working to watch this inconceivable betrayal. I walked to the front of the shop and waved at Nate and Hoarse as they drove off. Dad looked at me and my, "what the hell?" expression, went into his office and shut the door.

The guys stood frozen, perplexed, drained, having lost something they once had. Something they never knew they needed.

I watched Del pick up a hard rubber chew toy that resembled a light blue bone. He walked over to one of our galvanized trash cans, cursed and threw it in hard from about two feet away. The fuse was lit.

ONLY DEATH HAS NO REMEDY

Johnny Lazzara felt his blood pressure rise with the pitching of Rose's voice while the boys hunkered down in their bedroom. Sal had set her off earlier bringing home a note from his math teacher regarding three consecutive days of zeros. That was the tipping point. Roberto instinctively knew the line of fire was indiscriminate, so while Sal feverishly worked math problems like he was trying to win a war, Roberto shoved toys under the bed and into the back of the closet to make the place look neat. Johnny knew he was next, just as he knew the boys were paying for his indiscretion.

At dinner, Rose sat across the table building steam like a pressure cooker, while Johnny shoveled two servings of *ropa vieja* and white rice into his thick Sicilian frame. The boys tried to make themselves invisible. Sal with red eyes and shiny lines on his cheeks where tears had rolled. The silence held weight and made the air thick.

When Rose finished eating, she folded her napkin, placed it on the table too gently and left the kitchen without a word. Johnny cleared the table of what remained of dinner and filled the dishwasher, trying to time his exit and perhaps to assuage the inevitable.

In the living room, Rose stood in front of the television watching the scattered remnants of a space shuttle fall from the sky and folding laundry like she was trying to hurt it.

"I'm going to the shop," Johnny announced, pulling on a winter coat.

Rose turned to him and stood in the doorway with wet eyes. "What are we going to do, John?"

"End of the week," he said. "I need to finish a couple of jobs."

"And when they shut the power?" Rose said. "It's going to freeze tonight." She walked out of view for a moment and returned with a handful of envelopes which she placed on the kitchen counter in front of Johnny. She stood her ground for a moment, staring at him with palpable disappointment in her eyes, then she retreated into the other room.

"I've been back every night until eleven o'clock." Johnny spoke down the hall, but Rose had already shut the bedroom door. He could feel the color of his ears and the heat they produced. He thumbed through the envelopes printed in red ink. He looked at his blood pressure meds on the counter but decided that work was the medicine he needed. The shop was his church.

In the mudroom, between the carport and kitchen, Johnny removed his orthopedic slippers and slipped on his work boots, low tops, and he loosened the belt around the growing waistline of his khakis. The floor in the hall creaked and Johnny turned to see Rose in her night robe, arms crossed. "Don't forget your thermos," she said, as if it were an admonishment. "I made you café. And lock the door. Ybor City isn't what it used to be."

Johnny nodded sheepishly, grabbed his meds off the counter and walked out to the van, rocking side to side as he did, like a penguin into the night air beautiful and crisp. He looked to the clear, black sky and wondered if he should feel hopeful seeing the light of those stars shining through the darkness, or if it was darkness squeezing out the light. On the drive to Ybor City, NPR confirmed what Rose had said. It was going to freeze. He could feel it in his feet and in the toes that weren't there. When asked what happened to them, he'd say, "They just fell off one day." And he'd chuckle, making light of that truth, which would belie the bitterness of that memory, even thirty-five years on.

Johnny parked his van in front of the shop and listened to the thumping of music from the clubs on Seventh Avenue. He felt the heat in his ears with his fingertips. His blood pressure was dropping. At least he thought it was. Hoped it was. He could always take an extra pill. He grabbed the thermos and hopped out of the van, his mind already working. First, a bathroom vanity to finish. An hour's work, maybe two. The glue takes longer to dry in cold air. If he could deliver tomorrow, there would be money. A kitchen to cut. That would keep the men busy. Plenty of work and good money at the end of that. The shop was loaded with materials. He'd paid the supply house to keep the shop running, taking a gamble that jobs would be finished in time.

Light spilled onto the front of the building through the open front door, and the windows just under the roofline, glowed. There were no other cars in the parking lot. The garage doors were shut. Both Sarge and Pernell had keys to the place and often worked nights, but they would have said something.

Johnny studied the teeth marks on the doorframe and the splintered wood near his feet. A crowbar, he thought. One more thing to fix before he went home. If they took the tools, then what? He stepped into the shop and glanced through the office door, which had been kicked in. The office was an explosion of paper and blueprints. What held his attention though, was the tall, stringy figure in the center of the shop, leaning over the saw, staring into the sawdust in a peculiar way.

"What the hell are you doing in here?" Johnny said, before realizing it was Les, a guy who'd been on for a couple of months. Decent assembler but had no attention span. He wasn't a cutter. Les was in recovery, but not tonight. He spun around at the sound of Johnny's voice, wavering like a punch-drunk fighter. Hunched over, the way tall, skinny people often are. Jaw hung like a rabid dog. Three missing teeth. Eyes red. Oily hair hung over his ears. His skin pale, grayish in fact, covered in sweat and he looked as if he might pass out. This was more than alcohol.

Johnny recalled the day Les walked in the shop and figured he was a paycheck away from living in his car. But the man needed work.

An inch and a quarter piece of red oak was stuck in the saw, though it was off. The wood had bound between the blade and guide and threw Les's left hand into those screaming teeth. Johnny figured that out at a glance. He had the wrong blade in the saw and the guide in the wrong place. There were two fingers on the saw table and a large spattering of blood on the tabletop, up the wall and on the ceiling. The sound of drops hitting concrete drew Johnny's eyes to the ground next to Les's left foot, where a shiny red puddle reflected the white fluorescent lights. It seeped through the blood-soaked rag that Les had wrapped around his clenched fist. In his right hand, Les held a rifle, though it was facing the ground at the moment.

"That a Winchester .308?" Johnny asked, doing the math, judging the distance between himself and Les and the door.

"Yer god, damned right, Johnny," Les stuttered his words, raising the rifle with the assistance of his left fist, starting a new puddle in a new spot. "I want what's owed."

Johnny felt an odd calm fall over him. He smelled the burned wood from that dull blade and could see the remnants of sawdust hanging in the air under the fluorescents. It seemed that all those little specks were frozen in place. The switch to the saw was on. Must have popped the fuse when it bound. He didn't want to think about the cost of replacing that motor. He focused on Les. Not much you can do but be calm when you're staring at the barrel of .308. He'd felt that odd calm before, in another life, on a rocky, frozen ravine, north of the 38th Parallel.

The mortar hit twenty yards away sending body parts flying like a burst of popcorn. The cold air instantly freezing a mist of blood which floated down and speckled the muddy ice like red snow. Lazzara and Gutierrez, the two Marines from Ybor City, both barely out of their teens, were peppered with shrapnel and blown back to the icy ground. The sounds of war replaced with humming. Anguished shouts of Marines in their unit cut short. Johnny struggled to his feet. Gutierrez fought to his knees, but he couldn't rise.

Roberto Gutierrez was Cuban, and naturally, he and Johnny, having been acquaintances before the war, gravitated to each other. In Ybor City, everybody knew everybody. For Johnny, Roberto was a living breathing piece of home. He knew the language of Ybor City and the aroma on Seventh

Avenue of roasting coffee from Naviera. He knew the names of the men in town who evoked fear and commanded respect. He understood the perfection of a proper Cuban sandwich made with bread from La Segunda Bakery. And in their unit, only they understood why the smell of a good cigar transported them home. Both their families had come to this country at the turn of the century to roll cigars in Ybor City.

Johnny stepped in front of Roberto and fired his M1 at troops that had breached their line. Chinese from the 9th Army. The night before they'd bayoneted Marines in their sleeping bags. It was just the business of war. Tonight, they were back and pushing hard. The frozen air crackled in Johnny's sinuses which held the smell of gunpowder.

The place was the Chosin Reservoir. Thirty-thousand American servicemen surrounded by 120,000 Chinese troops. The odds were not as severe as the weather. Thirty-eight below at night with wind chills nearing sixty-below. Fifteen days in, Johnny had lost his ability to walk, but his unit was pinned, so he kept firing through the pain at men he didn't know. Now, powered by the will to live, he was up, and his right foot was simply numb. He fired at thin figures rushing toward them in the dark, aiming toward the white flashes of gunfire. Two groups of men shooting at faceless shadows. Johnny ran out of ammunition, picked up Roberto's rifle and continued firing up the rocky incline. Most of his weight on his left foot, balancing with his right. Roberto behind him, on his knees with his head bowed as if he were praying. There was shouting and constant reports of gunfire and explosions, but Johnny heard none of it. Only a dull hum. The earth shook as shells fell around their position caving a large section of the ravine, sending rocks, ice and men tumbling down the steep incline.

"Les, put that gun down" Johnny said, as if he were talking to one of his boys with a toy rifle. "Let's get you to a hospital maybe save those fingers." Johnny took a step and Les shoved the bolt in that Winchester forward and drew up the weapon. "You've been drinking or worse and you're not thinking straight."

Les leaned against the saw table and smacked his lips, like a man about to be sick.

"Everyone gets the same," Johnny said. "You'll get the rest when we deliver. Maybe Wednesday. Maybe Thursday."

"I'll take what you got."

"Well, if you shoot me, you get nothing," Johnny said, pulling out his wallet. He placed a five and two ones on the saw table while Les kept a bead on him with the rifle.

"Back away," Les said, looking at the money. "Shit." Les sunk and seemed bewildered.

"Gianni," a raspy old voice echoed in the shop. "*Mbare. Comu semu?*" The man spoke Sicilian.

Les looked beyond Johnny toward the voice and mumbled a string of incoherent expletives.

The old man entered the shop, clenching a fat cigar in his teeth and carrying a dovetail drawer under his arm. He was neatly dressed in dark gray slacks and black dress shoes with a crisp white shirt under a black, knee-length wool coat. Mostly bald with a scant of pure white hair combed straight back. His unstylish black glasses framed assertive eyes. The old man stopped ten feet behind Johnny and nodded as he surveyed the saw table massacre.

"Labor dispute?" The man continued speaking only in Sicilian, as Les drew a bead on him with that Winchester and screwed his face at the foreignness of the words. The old man put the drawer down, pulled the smoking cigar out of his mouth and spit. "Listen Gianni, Brancato is waiting outside. We can take care of this. It's not a problem."

"What the hell's he saying?" Les said.

"Santo," Johnny said, in Sicilian, waving his hands and ignoring Les. "*Tanti grazzi. No prublema.* He's drunk. Leave the drawer. I'll take care of it." Johnny stepped over, placing himself between the old man and the barrel of the Winchester. He was surprised to see Santo walk in his door. Like most people of means, he'd moved out of Ybor City years ago, but he kept his business offices nearby. Many of the historic brick buildings along Seventh Avenue were his. Their families went back a long way, though their association was little more than cursory.

In the silence between words, the thumping baseline from Seventh Avenue gave the shop a heartbeat that Johnny felt reverberating in his chest.

Les's face contorted with waves of pain and Johnny could tell the drugs and alcohol were wearing off. His movements were jerky, and his mind fogged with anguish. Johnny worried that Les would twitch from the pain before he passed out and send a round right through him. Of course, if he shot the old man, there would be no helping either of them.

"Les," Johnny said, speaking English. "We can remedy this situation. I don't need you pointing guns at my customers. It's bad for business."

"Ain't no remedy without settlement," Les said, spit flying through his missing teeth.

"*Sola la morte non c'e remedio*," Santo said to Johnny, who turned to Les wondering if he could save the man from his poor judgement.

"Talk English, goddammit," Les said.

Johnny heard the shouts of Chinese voices over the howling wind and he didn't need to understand the language to know the meaning. Their position was overrun. He tried to pull Roberto to his feet, but Roberto wouldn't budge. Other Marines were up and firing all directions.

"Get the hell out of here," Roberto said, as if it took all his energy to do so. "Leave me a loaded gun." He didn't realize, there was nowhere to go.

Backlit shadows appeared on the ridge above them and Johnny fired. Two bodies tumbled down the ridge. He saw a flash of white light and felt a sledgehammer hit his left shoulder. It spun him around on his way to the ground taking Roberto with him. Roberto fell face first over Johnny, with his lips nearly resting on Johnny's ear.

"Don't move," Roberto said.

Johnny looked up to that bone sky and wondered if there was a god impassively watching this melee and what he would say to him at this moment.

Chinese troops took more ground and Johnny felt a sharp pinch in his chest then the warmth of his and Roberto's blood pouring over him like a blanket. Roberto had been bayonetted in the back, and Johnny succumbed as the pain and cold coalesced into a singular apathy. He lay in surrender of it all, with tears freezing his eyes shut.

The Marines rallied and met the Chinese in a head on firefight which went on longer than Johnny was conscious. One Marine dove to the ground using their bodies for cover. He placed his M1 on Roberto's back and fired indiscriminately.

By morning, the two men were frozen together face to face like battlefield lovers. Roberto, a fallen statue. Frozen solid as if all his heat were transferred to Johnny. When medics cut the boot off of Johnny's right foot, three of his smaller toes broke off. They had turned black. The doctors saved his foot and Roberto had saved his life; a gift he could never repay. Johnny walked away from that frozen war carrying with him the burden of that debt.

"Gianni, if I may?" Santo said to Johnny in English, stepping from behind him to address Les directly. Johnny gestured with a palm in the air to acquiesce.

"You a married man?" Santo said to Les.

"Got an old lady," Les answered. "Tired of her bitchin. Tired a gettin' shit on."

Santo nodded. "My wife, she's been driving me crazy about this damned drawer. I walked out this morning and put it in my car. Point is, this circumstance presents an opportunity for you and for me."

Les looked to Johnny as if Santo were still speaking Sicilian.

"You'd be wise to listen," Johnny said, feeling powerless to help the man or himself.

"How much are you owed?" Santo said.

"Hunerd na quarter," Les slurred his words.

Santo put the cigar back in his mouth, pulled a crisp hundred out of his wallet along with a twenty and a five. He placed the money on the saw with Johnny's seven dollars and tapped on it with his fingers. Three taps. "Now, you've got what you came for. I've taken on his debt, so his business is with me."

Les swiveled his head between the money, the old man and Johnny, and he pursed his lips like he'd just lost a bet. "It was you shoulda paid," he said to Johnny.

Johnny stepped toward Les and put his hand out. In his other hand, he still held the thermos that Rose had prepared. "Did you come to shoot me, or did you come to get money?" Les handed Johnny the gun and grabbed the cash with his good hand. He turned and puked into the saw dust, wiped his mouth on his sleeve and stumbled toward the door, hunched over and moaning.

"Wait," Johnny said. "Take your fingers." He walked to the office and stashed the rifle. Then he dug into one of the desk drawers that Les hadn't turned over and grabbed a plastic baggy. He put ice cubes in the bag from the squat Westinghouse fridge, picked up the cold fingers and dropped them in. Johnny looked at the disembodied fingers, a middle and ring finger, and turned this over in his mind with Santo patiently watching and gnawing his cigar. "Les, did you lose another finger?"

"My pinky's in the sawdust," Les said, taking the baggy. "To hell with it. But I want ma huntin' rifle."

"I'll hold on to it for you," Johnny said. "You need a ride to the hospital?"

Les stumbled out the door.

Johnny turned his eyes to Santo. "He's just a drunk." Johnny said. "He won't be back. You'll never see him again."

The old man's mask of humor and gentility faded. "Your kids could have been here," Santo said and shrugged. "My grandkids. My wife. You understand."

Johnny nodded and said of course, but his mind raced. "Have some espresso with me. Let's take a look at that drawer. Things like this are fixable."

"I'm not so sure," Santo said, "but, pour me some and we'll talk." He walked coolly toward the open front door, pointed and said a few words in

Sicilian that Johnny couldn't hear. Then he ambled back to where Johnny stood holding their coffees in two Styrofoam cups with steam rising from them.

Johnny looked at Santo in a manner respectfully questioning the interaction.

"It's important he gets to the hospital," Santo said and gestured to the saw table and the ceiling. "There's a lot of blood here." He took one of the coffees from Johnny and raised it. *"Grazzi. Salud, chindon."*

The men downed their espressos and Johnny picked up the wobbly drawer and placed it on one of the low work tables for examination. "Anything can be fixed," Johnny said, studying the drawer. "It's nice work."

"It's not something I paid any mind to," Santo said, "until it became an annoyance. And when things become an annoyance, I get rid of them."

"It's a lot of trouble to go through, to get rid of something that you typically never even think about," Johnny said.

"Perhaps, but there's great satisfaction in having it gone."

"Santo, let me fix this," Johnny said, looking into the old man's eyes. "I'll bring it by tomorrow and I'll measure you for a whole new kitchen. You pay for the materials. The labor will cost you nothing. I'll design it and cover the expense."

Santo considered this silently, before saying, "Plus the hundred and twenty-five you owe me."

Johnny nodded. "Then maybe you can forget there was ever an annoyance."

The old man pulled the cigar from his mouth. "I appreciate what you did," Santo said, and Johnny assumed he meant stepping between him and the Winchester. "If it's important to you." Santo gestured his compliance.

Johnny nodded, and the men shook hands and with that, Johnny felt an ancient weight lifted. A debt paid.

"You saw what happened this morning?" Santo said. "Lives can end in so many ways. Surprising ways."

"It was on the news," Johnny said. "Terrible thing to look to the sky for hope."

Santo looked around the shop and filled his lungs, savoring the cool air. "This was good," he said, and patted Johnny on the shoulder. "Life already seems so much sweeter that we're still here to enjoy it."

Santo walked out and Johnny sat on the worktable next to the drawer and blew air out of his mouth which misted briefly then dissipated. He poured himself another espresso and took a sip thinking about what Les had said, "It was you shoulda paid." And he marveled at the irony of those words and the yoke of a debt that would never be paid.

UNDERCURRENT

Every summer, we spent a week at Indian Rocks Beach, about forty-five minutes from where we lived. Same motel. Same room. It had a beach and a pool, shuffleboard and a ping pong table. What more did we need?

The year I turned ten there were signs warning of riptide. The wind was calm, the sky blue and the water placid as glass. It was early in the day and there were a few people wading in the water and farther down the beach, kids splashing around in a shallow area. Locals with shoe-leather skin walked up and down the beach and tourists did the seaside stoop hunting shells. Gulls soared effortlessly against the warm gulf breeze and the buzzing of jet skis through the gulf added a grating tension. At the shore's edge, I watched fish darting in unison below the surface. My parents said not to go in beyond my waist. They watched me from shore while sneaking sips of Birra Moretti and rubbing lotion on their skin while my older brother followed bikinis up and down the beach. I stood in the cool water waving at my parents while the undertow tugged at my ankles, pulling me deeper into the Gulf. When the surface reached my neck, I stepped forward realizing I was in a fight. My father stood abruptly before I lost sight of him, my feet swept away, my body tumbling on the bottom, flailing, broken shells tearing my skin. My lungs burning. A wash of foggy green before my eyes. I was spun around, confused on which way to go. I swallowed salt water and breathed it into my lungs and thrashed beneath the surface. A leathery vice gripped my forearm and jerked me upward. The sun blinded me and cool air hit my skin. I wheezed and choked for air and spit up seawater on the bumpy ride to shore in my father's arms, while anxious onlookers gathered ankle deep in the water to gawk.

Later, I asked my father how he knew where to find me. He said he didn't.

The fight started right after lunch, at a time when the shop was usually quiet, with the guys sitting on our low work tables that were covered in dried glue and paint, eating Cuban sandwiches that my old man brought in, with the hum of the big fans carrying warm air through the shop stirring up sawdust into a wood scented cloud that sparkled in shafts of yellow sunlight and mingled in the air with our voices and laughter.

The boys were bullshitting about women while I walked around the shop with a clipboard and a calculator taking an inventory of materials and supplies. I'd finally graduated with a business degree eight months before and thought I'd take a shot at running the place. Thought I could change things, but my old man was a rock and rocks change very slowly, if at all. I stopped for a moment to listen to Del's story. Crazy shit always happened to Del and whether he was embellishing or not didn't matter. The stories were still funny.

Del said that before he'd met Eula, he'd picked up a waitress at the place where Eula danced and took her home. While he was working his way around in the dark, he ended up with a metal bar in his mouth. "It was attached to the end of her nipple," he said, "and I's like, what the hell?"

The guys laughed. Del was a lean dude, with curly blonde hair that was starting to gray, and he always wore safety glasses because he only had one good eye. The other he'd lost in a fight about five years back.

"I mean the last thing you'd expect is a piece of metal clanking on your fillings," Del said. "It was one of them metal bars, you know, with the round balls on the ends. Well one of them balls unscrewed and I swallowed it. I shit you not."

"What did you do?" Crazy Jimmy said. He'd stood there the whole time with his open mouth. He'd been married to Margie since he was eighteen. He talked to himself a lot and kept to himself, mostly.

"What'd I do?" Del smiled and paused for effect. "Hell, I rolled her over."

Even Fausto, one of our *marielitos*, laughed, and he barely understood English. Fausto stood behind the table saw mesmerized, waiting for the story to end so he could start cutting. Hard to know exactly how much of it he got. He always looked to be smiling because of ill-fitting dentures.

The guys stood and tossed their trash, and started back to work, when Donnie said, "So I was with two girls last weekend. Heh." This got our attention. Donnie had been at the shop about a week and was trying to fit in. Donnie. My cousin. My dad hired him, and I didn't have a say in the matter.

"Two," Del said, with a look of doubt.

"Heh, yeah," Donnie said. Donnie began and ended many of his sentences with, heh.

The guys turned with partial interest at what Donnie had to say and his face flushed. "Yeah. I was at this girl's apartment. And huh, she's on the bed with big, gazongas in my face. I like big girls. Heh."

"They make the rockin' world go 'round," Del said, laying out drawer faces on the work table so he could glue laminate on them.

"What's that supposed to mean?" Donnie said.

"Nothing," Del said, and shot me a look. I knew Del, and if you didn't know Queen you didn't know shit.

Crazy Jimmy appeared uncomfortable with the story but couldn't turn away. He was filing the edges of the countertop that he'd routed before lunch. Fausto, stood at the table saw with his finger on the switch, pausing out of machismo courtesy perhaps.

"So, I'm doing it and she's loving it, saying stuff like, 'thank you, Donnie, thank you, Donnie,' when the bedroom door opens and her friend, just like, walks in the room and says, 'I'll get in on some of that.' Heh. Know what she said? She said she wanted it from behind."

Donnie looked at Fausto, inserted his index finger into his closed fist and said, "*hasta el culo*," in a cracker accent.

Fausto looked at me and I shook my head. I'd known Donnie my whole life and there was more to this story than the surface revealed, but I let it playout. Everyone has to find their niche. Del's bullshit meter didn't have the same tolerance as mine.

"So," Del said, squinting his working eye, "is that when you closed your eyes and switched hands." Del made an obscene hand gesture that had us all laughing.

"You think I'm lying?" Donnie took a step toward Del and shoved him. "Nobody calls me a liar. You think I wasn't with a girl? Is that what you think?"

"What the fuck is wrong with you?" Del placed an opened hand on Donnie's chest, holding him away and looking over at me. Del was about five inches taller than Donnie who was pudgy and soft with an unpleasant paunch to his posture. He was pasty white and acted like a little old man even though he was seventeen. His hair was bristly and lopsided, and I had trouble looking at his face because he always had milky stuff caked in the corners of his lips. His father was a pudgy cracker who married my aunt and Donnie took after that side of the family. I knew he was medicated for some mental instability and an elongated acronym of some sort.

"Hey," I said and moved between them. I had Donnie by a few inches, and he felt fleshy and soft as I pushed him away. "Keep your fucking hands to yourself. This is a place of business. That happens again I'll toss you out of here."

"Uncle Johnny hired me, not you," Donnie shouted, his face crimson.

"Then be appreciative of that," I said, trying to channel the old man. I handed Donnie a rag and a bottle of mineral spirits and told him to clean the cabinets in the back of the shop, far away from Del.

"Robert, I don't give a shit if he's your cousin," Del said to me as we watched Donnie walk toward the back of the shop. "Just keep him away from me."

I said that Donnie was probably off his meds and Del chuckled at that, but I was serious. We watched Donnie drop the rag and bottle on a work table, walk out of the shop and put a finger to each of his nostrils to blow snot. Then he turned toward us, shouted, "Fuck you," and kicked one of the chickens that congregated behind the shop. There were feral chickens all over Ybor City. The bird squawked and hit the wooden fence with a thud.

Del tried to hold me back when he saw my intentions but didn't try very hard and gave up the effort. I walked out of the garage door toward Donnie who stood over the chicken watching it quiver. I pushed him aside and he took a wild swing at me. His fist glanced my jaw. I shoved him toward the fence with more force than necessary and he hit the back of his head on a four by four. He slid to the ground holding his head screaming. His hands damp with blood. My stomach turned. Not because of the blood, but because I thought I'd really hurt him.

"Del, get me some ice and a clean rag," I shouted into the shop. Crazy Jimmy and Fausto were frozen watching the spectacle. They weren't about to step in the middle of this shit. Del moved to the fridge with a chisel and a hammer. The squat little Westinghouse was frozen solid from a slow leak.

I tried to help Donnie up. He cursed, shoved me away and tried to kick me. I dropped to one knee, said we were getting ice and to let me take a look. There was commotion in the shop and the boys were talking. Fausto, rattling off in his staccato Spanish with his dentures clicking. I looked over to see a raging bull charging me. My old man. A thick, Sicilian, in his white T-shirt and Dickies. My greatest fear was that he was biting his tongue. He was. The result of a too short frenulum. If he drew blood I was fucked and I could see red in the corners of his mouth. He cursed in Italian and shoved me away and I tumbled to the ground. He lifted Donnie up like the boy was made of paper. Del showed with a chunk of ice, wrapped in clean white cloth and Dad held it to the back of Donnie's head and helped him into the shop with Donnie saying, "He doesn't like me. Why doesn't he like me?"

Blood spread into the rag like ink on a white table cloth and I knew there was no explaining this shit to the old man.

"Sorry, Robert," Del said, extending a hand to help me up. "I shoulda let it slide. I know that kid ain't right."

I looked over at the chicken, jerking intermittently, grabbed a shovel to sever the bird's head and then buried it behind the shop, just below the surface.

Beyond having small talk about sports or the weather while paying for a six pack or a bottle of Chianti, I'd never had much conversation with the guy at the liquor store. But I found myself at the counter getting tutored on the puzzling story of Angostura bitters.

I'd been interviewing for jobs behind the old man's back, months before he hired Donnie. A software company had me in three times and there was an offer on the table. It was a life changer. One afternoon, while secretly getting my interview haircut, I read in one of those men's magazines that the Old Fashioned was the classic American cocktail for white collar professionals. So instead of buying wine or beer, I bought bourbon and a bottle of Angostura bitters, two of the ingredients. The other two ingredients were sugar and a slice of orange.

"What's in it?" I said to the guy behind the counter handing him the little white bottle. Except for the two of us, the store was empty. The sun had set and I was still in my glue stained blue jeans and work boots and covered in sawdust.

"It's a mystery," he said, scanning the barcode. He then went into a dissertation of sorts on how the exact combination of herbs and spices was shrouded in secrecy by the family who created it.

"Only five people in the world actually know the ingredients and they have vowed never to be in the same room or on the same airplane together."

I didn't give the story much credence, but it reminded me that people were mysteries. Everybody was hiding something.

I took the job and told them I had to give two weeks. Ten days had passed and I hadn't told the old man, nor had I opened the bottle of bourbon. It never seemed to be the right time. So, my cousin Donnie took a swing at me, I shoved him out of frustration and now I sat in the red chair next to my old man's desk picking at the spongy yellow cushion that burst through cracks in the vinyl. My dad's white handkerchief was crumpled on the desk. It was spotted with blood from where he'd bitten his tongue. He was pounding on the calculator with his thick fingers like he was pissed off at it.

"The boy's got problems," he said, not looking at me. "They were afraid to admit that something was wrong. But you," he stopped to point at me, "*teste di cucuzza*, you should know better. The boy needed stitches and it's coming out of your pay."

I stared at the rug on the office floor with no desire to make eye contact. The rug was speckled with bits and pieces of wood and mica from every job we'd ever done. Counting them all would be a life sentence.

"What do I tell my sister?" he said.

"He shouldn't be here," I said. "He hasn't got the temperament or the aptitude for the work."

"When you have a shop, you run it the way you want," he said. "That's it. No more. He's your cousin. He works here."

I felt pressure building inside me and it had nothing to do with Donnie, and everything to do with things like Donnie. I looked across the desk and stared at two empty cigar boxes and I knew at that moment that a confrontation was unavoidable and long overdue. The old man paid everybody under the table, never saved receipts or wrote off any expenses. All I asked him to do was to put receipts in one box and expenses in the other and I'd figure out the rest, but the only thing in those boxes was dust. I was up to my neck with the current pulling at my ankles, and it seemed easier to pick a fight than to tell the truth. The truth was premeditated, a slap in the old man's face. It would do more damage than a punch in the gut.

Sometimes the right thing to do isn't the best thing to do.

"You're throwing money away and I can't fucking stand it anymore," I said, and stood over him. This got his attention. I'd never cursed directly at the old man, not like that. "I can't even get you to save receipts and invoices and you wonder why this shop is always struggling."

"We'll start next year," he said.

"You want me to run this shop, change starts now. And Donnie goes or I go."

He bit his tongue and slapped his hand on the desk. He said, "You've looked out that door like a *mammoni* for fifteen years. You want to go? Go."

Mammoni means momma's boy and he knew that would cut deep, because it wasn't true. He was right about one thing. I'd thought about this day from the time I was in my teens, buoyed and imprisoned by familial obligations. "I quit then," I said. "Run the business the way you want. I can't do it anymore."

I took a step toward the door and he grabbed my forearm. "Roberto," he said, and pulled me back. His eyes were ancient and held the expression of a punch-drunk fighter who didn't know when to quit. I shook my head, pulled my arm away and said I had to do something different.

Fresh air hit my face when I walked out of the garage door and I became dizzy with freedom, walking from the shop fearful and hopeful. At my car, I looked back at the shop and watched the evening guys working under the bright fluorescent lights. My internal compass was off kilter. I didn't know what I wanted in this world.

That evening, in my Seminole Heights apartment, surrounded by tongue-and-groove cedar walls that smelled of yesterday, I opened that bottle of bourbon and drank it on ice. It burned all the way down.

The weekend before I started my new job, I went to Ybor City with a couple of buddies. It was the place where my family had settled when they came from Sicily at the turn of the century. Now it was a bar district lined with century old red brick buildings. We stopped at a corner next to a gay bar waiting for the light to turn so we could cross over Seventh Avenue to the Irish Pub. While waiting for a break in the traffic, I glanced back at the crowd lined up in front of the bar. People were laughing loudly and talking over the music. Some of the guys were dressed in drag, they were dancing on the sidewalk, the house music vibrated in my chest and everyone seemed to be having a good time. Some of the men had breasts or implants and wore revealing outfits and that wasn't something you see every day. They wore low cut dresses to reveal their cleavage and had big bouffant hair-dos with knee high boots like that singer from The B-52's. I tried not to look but couldn't help myself. Something caught my eye and my buddies caught me staring.

"Aye Rob, you biting the fucking pillow now?" one of them said, and they both laughed and started across the street, but I didn't move. Fuck them. They were idiots.

I stood there and watched a guy tonguing what looked to be a portly woman with big tits. What caught my eye was that the woman wasn't a woman and the other guy was my cousin, Donnie. He was wearing a coat and a bowtie. His hair was slicked back and he looked like a character out of the movie *Casablanca*. He didn't see me at first, and I guess I never really saw him.

Then Donnie looked my direction and caught me staring, so I walked over, and he stepped away from the dude in the dress.

"How's the back of your head?" I said and I shook his hand.

"Fine. I got four stitches," he said. "I didn't know you cared so much about those chickens." He chuckled.

"Yea," I said, "neither did I."

The Hygienist

Eula took a moment between patients to rub both sides of her jaw with her middle and index fingers and stared at one of the drawers in the exam room. She'd peed on the stick right after her last patient and the results awaited her there in the dark. The hinge in her jaw ached from clenching. The phone buzzed and the receptionist said her next victim had arrived, then giggled. The drawer could wait.

On her way to the door, the patient mirror attracted Eula's eyes. It had been that way since the days when there was reciprocity between her body and physical currency, which at one time meant survival. She admired the shine of her flat-ironed, bottle-black hair and extensions, and bared her ultra-white teeth; a benefit of working for a cosmetic dentist. She placed a hand on her belly and frowned, recalling what pregnancy had twice done to her body and what it would do again with so many ifs attached to that thought.

Eula's next client was Robert, a guy she'd heard about for years and met for the first time at her wedding last month. Robert grew up at the cabinet shop where Del worked and fronted up at their wedding with his parents. Robert was married to a girl named Cheryl, a trust fund baby from what Eula gathered, but he came to the wedding without her.

Robert hugged Eula in the lobby, and she smiled as if still floating on her honeymoon high, even though she and Del had been together on and off for going on twenty years and their relationship was more a habit than anything else. Robert was a polite hugger. She remembered that from the wedding. Eula had the kind of chest that turned heads and most guys wanted to feel her bust full-on, but Robert chose to give her a side hug, maybe out of deference to Del. Eula still thought it polite as hell. It was a long needy hug, though, and it made Eula wonder if Robert knew about her past or perhaps had a picture in his mind of her younger body beneath the sky-blue dental smock, which was pressed flat and flared away from her birthing hips like a tent.

At the reception, which took place at the neighborhood civic center that smelled of old wood and pine cleaner, Eula mentioned that she was a dental hygienist and right away Robert said he had a toothache and pointed to the side of his mouth. He was a man, so it took him a month to make the appointment. Now he was in her chair holding a consternated expression.

"Did you and Del go on a honeymoon?" Robert said in the same nasally voice as his father. The whole family had big noses and deviated septums, Eula surmised.

"If you could call it that," Eula said, opening Robert's mouth, which held the faint scent of garlic and which caused a brief wave of nausea. She stepped away pretending to organize her dental mirror, curette and sickle scaler on the counter behind her, and held it together, wondering if the drawer would confirm what she already suspected. She could almost feel the cells dividing in her uterus. Eula breathed deeply through her nose and focused on the remains of a gift basket on the counter which consisted of once beautiful crotons and calla lilies, now brown, shriveled from neglect.

"Del and I took the boys down to Siesta Key for a long weekend," she finally said. They had all fished and Del drank too much beer. Their boys, Carl and Delbert, were thirteen and twelve, twenty-months apart, though only one of them, the younger one, was Del's kid.

JOSEPH ALLEN COSTA

Robert's teeth were stained to hell from coffee and red wine, which he admitted to indulging in, but they were straight, flossed, and fairly-well brushed. "When was the last time you had a cleaning?" Eula said. Robert shrugged. "Your gums are in good shape, but you're grinding your teeth like the world's coming to an end."

"Life stuff," he said. "Sicilians worry. It's genetic. This one hurts." Robert tapped one side of his jaw and opened his mouth.

"You need a mouth guard," Eula said, looking at Robert's teeth. "My grandmother used to say, worry was like having drunk monkeys scamper through your brain in the middle of the night. You can't control'em, so you might as well let them go." Eula touched the L-2 molar with the sickle scaler and Robert stiffened like his body had taken a jolt of electricity. He uttered an expletive and then apologized.

"That's the one," Eula said without empathy. "You cracked this filling and let it go a while. Let something like this go, it starts to decay from inside out."

"Think we'll have to pull it?" Robert said.

"You need X-rays," Eula said. "Might get by with a root canal and save the tooth."

171

Eula said she'd give his teeth a proper cleaning, get x-rays, and then call the dentist for a look-see. "Problems tend to grow when you ignore them," she said, then realizing the irony of her words, glanced at the drawer and clenched, wondering if the contents would explode her life into pieces. Then, for the briefest of moments, Eula walked through the steps she would take to end the pregnancy and keep it a secret. It was only a thought, but the solution had merits, including keeping her body, her job, and her husband. A millisecond later, she'd already done it, at least in her mind, and felt the immense weight of the aftermath.

Del Murphy had walked out on Eula four times. The first time he was gone about three months. She was still dancing at the time. Del said it was too much too fast for him. Eula gave up on him and Carl was the result of that interlude. That, and a good-looking black man that Eula had one night with. There was no hiding it when the boy was born since Del was tall, fair, and sinewy. He saw that baby and walked out again. He came back a week later. The third time was eight years ago, while Eula was going to school to get her hygienist certificate. Del was cooking up a big money deal trying to sell pot so he could open a shop in his father's garage. That was his escape plan. Had he succeeded then, he'd have paid Eula some money and taken off for good. Eula couldn't let that happen and took steps to make sure it didn't. The boys needed a father and at the time, she needed Del.

Before Del up and proposed, with a gold band and everything, he took off again. This time for two months. All his clothes smelled of sawdust and Eula suspected he was crashing over at Johnny's cabinet shop.

"I'm not letting you come back this time, Del Murphy," Eula said, and thought she meant it when she heard the words come out of her mouth. She'd seen Del's picture on Facebook with his arms around a twenty-something at a bar called Good Time Charley's. Del denied that anything happened, but the euphoric expression on his stupid face set her off. It wasn't so much that Del was flirting with a girl half her age. It was his expression that got to her. When Del crawled back this time, he fronted up with a ring and a proposal.

Eula knew he'd be back or suspected as much. But if he could go off and fool around, why couldn't she? To Eula's thinking, men and women had a trade-off of needs that came with a certain amount of abnegation. Men wanted sex. Women wanted tenderness. They both gave up something to get what they wanted.

"Life stuff?" Eula said, using the tartar scraper on Robert's teeth. "Does it have something to do with you coming to the wedding without your wife?"

Robert looked at Eula and nodded. She used the saliva ejector to suck out the debris that she'd scraped away. The ongoing issue, Robert said, was that he hated his job, but that his father-in-law owned the company.

"So, your marriage is tied to your job and you can't leave one without losing the other," Eula said, feeling the urge to solve the problem, any problem.

"Something like that," he said.

"Any kids?" Eula said focusing on his front teeth which were beginning to whiten. Robert shook his head and Eula said that kids complicate things. "But I love my boys. I couldn't imagine life without them." Then a thought occurred to her. "Do y'all want kids?" She pulled her hands out of his mouth so he could answer. Robert's eyes darted from her bust, which hung right in his face. Even a gentleman's eyes will take a walk now and again.

"You sound like my mother," Robert said. He opened his mouth and Eula went back to work, polishing his teeth with the prophylaxis and paste. Robert's mood shifted after that. He stared at the wall and seemed disengaged. He crossed his legs and his arms lying in her chair.

"Long as you're both on the same page," Eula said. "If not, that's a problem."

Robert nodded his head, perhaps thinking that he gave nothing away, but Eula saw through his silence as if the answer itself were a screaming baby.

Eula thought about the day she delivered Carl. She was young and stupid and sometimes went days without taking her birth control. She went natural and the contractions were hard, but she wanted all her faculties when the boy came out, just in case it was obvious that the boy wasn't Del's. The stamp of that moment was as indelible. Eula remembered it like she was a bystander watching her own delivery. She lay on the table with her knees up and her legs spread, while the nurse, doctor and Del stared at Christmas waiting for magic to happen. They were happy, the three of them, while she struggled to push that boy out. She recalled the euphoric moment, when the doctor placed Carl on her chest. He was warm and wet on her skin and his baby smell intoxicated her. Through the blur of tears, she looked at Del to share the moment but his face held the stunned expression of an innocent man having been awarded a death sentence. If there had been a hole somewhere the doc might have crawled into it. He looked at the baby and back at Del. The nurse didn't miss a beat.

"Congratulations," the nurse said. "He's a precious miracle."

After she and Del were left alone, all Eula could think to say was, "Well what did you expect? You were gone three months."

She'd had complications with Delbert's delivery and afterward the doctor said that if she got pregnant again it'd be a miracle. It would also be a high-risk delivery. Now, the whine of the prophylaxis on Robert's teeth echoed through the room and she thought that would be some damned miracle. A precious little wrecking ball.

Eula had more life experience than most and believed she could assess people's lives in a way they couldn't themselves. People wanted to be told what to do even if they knew the answer. Problem was, most didn't have the sand to make the hard decisions necessary to better their predicaments, like the battered woman who won't leave her man. Eula was stronger than that. She'd been there, before Del came along. She'd nursed bruises on her face, lived in her car at one time, raised two boys with and without Del's help, danced naked in front of men for money and endured it all to put herself through school and find a respectable job. She knew how to make hard decisions, like souring Del's big money deal by calling the cops. Del had lucked into a pile of wild growing pot and was in with some nasty bikers to sell it. Eula waited until Del was away from the house where the weed was stashed and she called in an anonymous tip. The cops busted the bikers and took all the pot. Del had no choice but to come back to her and the boys and go back to his regular job at Johnny's cabinet shop.

Robert confessed that his wife didn't want kids and Eula offered the hard advice she thought he needed.

"You ever read *National Geographic*?" she said.

"Sometimes," Robert said, touching his cheek on the side with the bad tooth.

"The doc's got all those magazines out in the lobby, and at lunch time I usually pick one up to read. Well, I read about this guy named Cortés who sailed to Veracruz, Mexico in the fifteen-hundreds. When they got there, he gave orders to burn the ships. Said it would motivate the men."

"He burned his ships?" Robert repeated.

"You make a decision like that," Eula said, "well, that's taking control of the matter. That's a commitment."

Eula stood aside as Dr. Ahmad, a tall, good looking black man with long, slender fingers and manicured nails, examined Robert's teeth. Eula put a hand on the doctor's shoulder and asked if he needed the X-rays. He smiled and eyed Eula's breasts, saying thank you. She enjoyed that moment and knew she still had something special. Something men wanted. Something Ahmad wanted. Something, it seemed that Del could take or leave. The doc was a married man and she was a married woman and there was comfort in that invisible wall that lay between them. A pretense that would crumble under a baby's cry.

"We can maybe save this tooth with a root canal," Dr. Ahmad said, studying the X-rays.

"Pull it," Robert said, looking at Eula.

"But," the doctor protested, "if I can save the tooth."

"Pull it and replace it. Put in an implant," Robert said. "I want it gone."

"I'm certified as an oral surgeon and we can do the work now, but are you sure that's what you want?" Dr. Ahmad said.

"Do it," Robert said.

The doc said fine, asked Eula to prep for the extraction and walked out to see other patients.

"Burn the ships," Robert said to Eula after the doc had gone.

"Burn the ships," Eula repeated, feeling buoyant.

"Yep," Robert said. "And I've got a whole book of matches."

COMETS

Eula felt a sudden kinship with Robert and felt his decision had larger implications than the rotten tooth. She glanced at the drawer with the urge to resolve her own dilemma. The way Eula figured it, if the test were positive, she had about six months and a fifty-fifty shot at Del being a daddy again, or a stepdaddy, or she could set a match to it all and walk away.

Eula walked Robert out with gauze stuffed in his mouth to absorb the blood. He would have to come back in a few weeks for his new tooth. She told the receptionist she'd need a few minutes before the next patient and went back into her exam room and shut the door. She stood directly in front of that drawer, put her hand on the knob, then looking at the dead gift basket on the counter, threw the plants in the trash.

Jenny was a long-time patient in for her bi-annual cleaning. Upon seeing Jenny in the lobby, Eula froze and smiled. She watched how the other patients fawned over her and her maternal stature and she recalled the attention received with both her pregnancies.

"How far along are you?" Eula said

"Eight and a half months," Jenny said, waddling toward the exam room.

"You look amazing," Eula said, and gave Jenny a side hug and thought again about having a newborn placed on her chest, that new baby smell and she had the strangest nipple sensation of breast feeding.

"He's kicking," Jenny said, with a hand on her belly. "You want to feel it?"

"I do," Eula said, placing her palm on Jenny's belly. "I absolutely do."

Involuntary Memory

The floor creaked in the hall outside my bedroom at 3:20 in the morning, and shortly after that, the doorknob quietly turned. I had a Louisville slugger in my hands and a hundred-pound dog snoring next to my bed. On the other side of the door was Mike Harper, a childhood friend who had suffered a mental breakdown, thought mobsters were after him, was carrying a large knife and pining away for Adeline, a woman he hadn't seen in a dozen years.

I set up three feet from the door, doing my best Pete Rose, ready to bash his face in. The bat slid wet in my palms. Sweat tickled my back. The doorknob squeaked. I set my stance and saw my moonlit shadow winding up against the wall for a homerun swing. Playing it through my mind, I wondered what it would it sound like. I wondered where the blood would go.

Mike had been a good friend, but if he came through that door there was a good chance I'd kill him.

I'd arrived home from my shop early, brewed coffee, and watched a bright shaft of sunlight in my living room get winnowed away by a fat gray cloud. It was late afternoon and the sky dimmed in anticipation of a front. As soon as I moved toward the window, Dash, my yellow lab, was on his feet nuzzling me with the kind of loyalty unique to dogs. I scratched his head and opened the blinds fully, filling the room with bluish light. Across the street jack-o'-lanterns with the carved faces of comedy and tragedy stared at me from the neighbor's porch. I sipped coffee and watched a stray calico bury shit in my cypress mulch. The phone rang. It was Mike calling to dredge up the past.

Forty-five minutes later, I pulled into Union Station and looked for that familiar face among scattered groups of people bound together under umbrellas. Through the wipers and the raindrops, I saw a man who resembled Mike, but this guy had a distended stomach, a bloated face and receding wavy hair. He wore what looked to be an expensive suit, white shirt and no tie, and he floated through the parking lot with his head high and his nose up.

"Mike," I said, assessing what the years had done. "It's been a long time." I shook his hand, which was soft and slender.

"There were people watching me in the train station," he said. His eyes darted nervously. "Two old guys in suits."

"Why would people be watching you?" I said.

"People have agendas," he said. "We'd better get out of here." He smiled awkwardly revealing yellow teeth. I smelled alcohol on his breath and noticed that his eyes were glassy and red. I opened the rear hatch and tossed in his beat-up leather bag.

He clambered into the passenger seat. "What did you do, crawl here?"

"I said forty-five minutes."

"I lost my cell phone," he said, then turned quickly to look out the passenger window and then through the side view mirror as I pulled away.

Mike smelled unwashed and had a few days of beard growth. He looked around at the interior of my new Jeep Cherokee and said, "When I lived in Europe I drove a Mercedes SUV. You wouldn't believe how tight that motherfucker was. German precision tolerance is measured in micrometers."

"I was surprised to get your call," I said, and turned the air up a notch. "I thought you'd fallen off the earth."

Mike nodded as if there were more to say. He didn't rent a car because his mother wasn't driving anymore and he needed to pick up her Buick.

"Adeline and I split up," he blurted out. "She took everything. She took my soul."

Sins and secrets reside in shallow graves, and at that moment, I regretted having picked up the phone and I regretted Mike's presence here.

"Have you spoken to her?" I said.

Mike tugged at his bottom lip, a tic he always had, and he shook his head. "Things have changed," he said, and stared through the passenger window at the endless line of strip malls and restaurants. He appeared perplexed by it all, like an alien studying a landscape of concrete and fluorescent lights that blurred into hues of color in the wetness and fading light.

We drove to the cadence of the windshield wipers and the rain and there was an uncomfortable silence that filled the space between us.

"How long has it been since you've been home?" I said.

He shook his head and said, "I need a drink."

When we got back to my house, I turned all the lights on so Mike could see the place. I pulled two beers out of the fridge and Mike asked if I had something stronger with Dash thumping his rebar tail against the wall and jumping all over him. "There's a bottle of vodka in the cabinet next to the fridge," I said.

I told Dash to lie in his bed and he did, but he kept a cautious eye on Mike.

"Vodka from Texas?" Mike scoffed and poured a hefty glass with some ice and tapped it to my beer. "Did you buy the house like this?" He looked around and it made me feel good.

"No, I spent a year renovating. Did every bit of it myself. I refinished the hardwood floors, re-plastered the walls and built new cabinets as they did back in the twenties. It's listed on the National Historic Registry." He looked around and nodded, plopped himself down on the couch and immediately lowered the blinds. Rain fell hard and tapped on the windows like a thousand strangers.

I choked up on the bat and thought about pitching those round summer melons in high school, swinging for the cheap seats and laughing like hell with my friends. The melons exploded, sending red flesh all directions. I stared at the bedroom door. It was one of the originals, from 1920; a sturdy door, with a crystal doorknob that sparkled in the moonlight. The door creaked behind Mike's weight. Sweat dripped into one of my eyes and burned. My breathing got shallow and the room closed in.

What part had I played in the events that led to this moment? Did he know about me and what I'd done, or was I paranoid? I knew the kind of monster he was and what had occurred so many years ago, and I wanted to hurt him for it.

I thought about Mike and the day our friendship ended, and stepped into my resolve, waiting for his face to show through that door.

One summer, before Adeline, Mike and I went to meet two girls. Mike and the girls were in their mid-twenties. I was in college. One of the girls brought out four glasses of sweet tea and we sat by their apartment pool under the shade of an umbrella and for that afternoon we were rich. It was a hot day and the tea was cold and the girls were curvy and sexy in their bikinis and they were smoking menthol cigarettes. Mike and the girls were laughing about a joke I wasn't in on. Then he looked at me and said, "Listen, don't freak out, but we put something in the tea. LSD." I knew he was serious. I was pissed and my stomach knotted. I didn't want that shit in my body. They were all talking at once and saying how much fun we were going to have. One of the girls flashed me and the three of them laughed even harder. I started to calm down and the world began to warp. Things all seemed to move differently. Slower. The familiar became peculiar. Then Mike said it was going to last six to seven hours and there was nothing I could do about it and that I needed to stay cool, have fun and ride it out. Six to seven hours of hallucinating, laughing, crying, huddled in a corner scared, wondering when it was going to end. I avoided Mike's calls for more than a year after that. Then he called and offered a half-assed apology for what had happened and asked me to meet him and his fiancée at a wine bar.

I rattled up in my Falcon with the $95 Earl Scheib paint job and parked next to Mike's new BMW. Mike wore a coat and tie and flashed money and introduced me to Adeline. She was an emergency room nurse, an RN, with a crazy, unapologetic laugh. When she spoke, she placed her hand on my arm in a way that made me feel as if I'd known her for years. Her brown hair was pulled back into a functional ponytail and she had a round, freckled face with soft, caramel eyes. There was a sizeable marquise diamond on her finger with a silver band. Mike doted on her and I couldn't blame him. I liked her instantly and I think the feeling was mutual. I watched them together, and I looked at his car and his suit and his trajectory and I wanted what he had. I was there for his benefit, so I could see him in his glory. That was the last time I saw Mike, until he showed up at the train station.

We'd grown up looking over the fence and wanting, and suddenly he was on the other side looking back.

Fear of the unknown is debilitating. Did Mike have the knife behind that door? Was he here to make me pay for what I'd done? I glanced at the clock. It was 3:21. Dash nudged my leg and growled. I quietly shushed him, thinking that we'd have the advantage of surprise. I squeezed the bat and rubbed on the knuckle I'd broken the night Mike and the girls had drugged me, with no recollection of how it occurred, except for having been told that I'd punched a hole through a wall in an imaginary

fight, and it occurred to me that I had not forgiven
him for that night or for his success.

We sat in my living room with our drinks. I sipped
beer and Mike drank my vodka. Dash barked and
Mike sprung from his seat. "Is someone here?" He
peered through the blinds and scanned the street.

"Relax," I said. "Dogs hear shit and they bark."

Mike called the shop when he arrived, and my
dad gave him my number. He asked how my old
man was doing and I said work makes him happy.

"I'm surprised you're still there," he said.

"You and me both," I said, letting his
condescension slide. "I ended up with a business
degree and quit, but went back five years ago,
because I wanted to." I told Mike that we had eight
craftsmen working for us now and were building
custom signature pieces; all hardwoods, cherry,
birch, sapele, and mahogany. "We have a website
and we're picking up projects all over the country.
I travel around looking for aged woods from
century-old farmhouses."

"A website." He chuckled. "Good for you guys.
And you're single?"

"I had a starter marriage. She wanted to travel the world and drink champagne and well, I wanted to build furniture."

"When'd you get divorced?"

"Five years ago."

He took a long swig of vodka and said, "Man, we were knee deep in it back in the day."

Truth of the matter was, Mike always picked up the girls, especially the ones that traveled in pairs. I'd usually get the castoff. Which wasn't altogether a bad deal.

"But, I'd do anything to get Addy back," he said. "She kept me grounded. We had a misunderstanding. I think I just need to . . . have you seen her?"

I shook my head and thought about Adeline. "We never traveled in the same circles," I said, and asked him about Italy.

"In the afternoons, I'd walk up to the Piazza di Spagna, get a glass of wine, sit on the Spanish Steps and watch happy couples throw coins into Trevi Fountain."

The light from a car illuminated the blinds.

"Shit!" Mike turned quickly and looked through the blinds for a long moment then turned back toward me with startled eyes, his hands trembling.

"Jesus, Mike. It's just the pizza." I said, over Dash's barking.

Mike reached for his wallet as I headed for the door, then explained that he only had credit cards and helped himself to a second glass of vodka. Another fat pour.

The pizza guy, a middle-aged Hispanic man, kept diverting his eyes over my shoulder toward Mike, who eyed him suspiciously from the kitchen.

"Did you know that guy?" Mike asked when I walked in with the pizza.

"It's just a guy who delivers pizza," I said.

"Everyone hides in plain sight," he said.

Under the track lighting in the kitchen, I noticed that Mike's suit was frayed at the edges. When he turned, I noticed a discoloration on the back of the coat. A stain about the size of a fist.

"Nice suit," I said, when he caught me looking.

"I had this tailored in Rome." He opened one side of the coat with his thumb and index finger so I could see a large custom label sewn inside. "One hundred percent Italian silk. Bought the loafers there too." He raised a leg to show me his soft leather shoes with heels worn to wedges by years of abrasions. "When you purchase clothes of high quality instead of buying crap off the rack they're going to last you and wear better."

Mike excused himself to change while I dished out the pizza. I watched him walk away and thought about a story I'd read in one of those pop-psychology books. The story told of a seven-foot tall statue of a Greek youth that the Getty Museum was going to purchase for millions of dollars. Experts studied the piece for a year and declared it genuine. Then one historian, in a glance, declared it a fake for no other reason than it just didn't look right.

Mike came back from the bedroom wearing worn jeans, slip-on sneakers and the same white shirt now untucked. The pits of his shirt were discolored. He popped four pills in his mouth and swallowed them with what was left of his vodka. "Steroids and a couple of stress relievers," he explained. "Gout. That's how they're treating it. They've bloated me up like the Hindenburg." He rubbed his ample stomach and asked how I stayed so thin, and I told him that I was still a runner and got lucky genes.

We sat at the kitchen table and Mike ate like an empty man. "Do you know the pain of loss?" he asked. "Or of blind injustice?"

"We all grieve in different ways," I said, and told him of my failed marriage. I'd worked for a Fortune 500 company. It paid well, but I hated it. Every day I went to work and stared at a shitty desk and a computer screen. One day I looked at my hands and felt as if I'd thrown away a gift. "You ever want something so badly that you'd lose your soul to get it?"

Mike nodded. "So, you quit," he said.

"Her father owned the company."

When I asked what brought him back home and if it was to see Adeline, Mike stood abruptly and helped himself to another vodka. His third in the past hour. He filled up the glass, then he went into the living room to peer through the blinds. He paced oddly, the way a person does when they want to say something or do something. He shook his head and ran a hand through his wavy hair, which made him look wild and unsteady. And he stumbled through this story of having worked for an import-export business in Jersey. He said they had a lot of cash coming in and going out. He suspected they were laundering money and that they would bury him because he knew too much. I pressed him for details, but he offered none.

"And you think they followed you here?" I said.

"I'm ready for them." From under his shirt, he pulled out an old hunting knife with a ridiculously long blade. The blade was not shiny, nor did it appear sharp, and the tip was blunted flat, as if it had been chipped on something hard. "I'll cut their fucking balls off. I'll kill those motherfuckers." He waved the knife in the air. "Do you have a gun in the house?"

I shook my head and put down my beer. Mike downed his vodka the way I down water after a run and he headed back to the kitchen to finish what was left of the bottle, still clutching that knife. He filled the glass, dropped in a cube of ice and took a long swallow. I was watching the man poison himself. The pills and vodka had done their work. Mike staggered around my kitchen with that goddamned knife. Even Dash thought he was crazy and cocked his head sideways to watch Mike. I got a sickly feeling in my gut.

"Anyway," Mike said, staring at the plantation shutters, "I figured I'd get the hell out of there and come down here and maybe find Adeline and talk to her. Just talk. All I wanted to do was talk to her, right, but, but she wouldn't give an inch. Not a fucking inch. You wouldn't give." He screamed at the shutters. His face became a ruddy tomato that seemed as if it would burst. His hand white-knuckled around that knife, while I sat as passively as I could at the kitchen table.

"When was the last time you spoke to her?" I said, in an overly calm voice. Dash moseyed up wagging his tail and rested his head in my lap, perhaps sensing my uneasiness. I felt naked and defenseless.

Mike turned sharply as if he just realized I was there. He slurred words in disjointed sentences and gestured violently with that knife. "She's. That whore. Call-blocked me. Had a restraining order on me. On me? Said I hurt her. She wanted it. She asked for it. It was an accident. Then, I went out of town and, on business you know, and when I came back. If she had come to Italy. I know she was fucking somebody. She wouldn't commit. She was always flying back home. Flying back home. Flying back home." His voice trailed off. He drank the vodka and wavered as drunks do. His eyes seemed at that moment to look through me. He sat and held the knife on the kitchen table and rocked as if in a trance.

I knew Adeline had been flying back home, because she told me herself while we were in bed together.

I ran in the crisp air that morning, feeling alive and strong, treading light-footed over fallen leaves. I should have known better. I slipped on those leaves as if on ice and ended up in the ER to be nursed by a bubbly RN whose face lit up upon seeing mine.

Adeline wore a colorful silk scarf around her neck to prevent the stethoscope from irritating her skin, so she said. I learned later, that was a lie.

We met for drinks and ended up at her apartment; me with stitches in my knee from a sprinkler head. She told me that Mike had moved to Jersey and that she had visited him a few times but had not quit her job nor given up her apartment. She was not wearing the engagement ring.

"Mike drinks," she said to me. "He drinks a lot, and he takes Xanax for anxiety and when that doesn't work he takes other drugs. He gets violent. You're the only friend of his I've ever met. That's weird, right?"

We talked late into the night and drank a lot and we laughed, giddy, drunk, guilty laughs. When she removed the scarf, I saw bruises on her neck, and I touched them.

"He's not the same," she said.

I shared the LSD story and showed her the lump on my knuckle, to justify what I knew was going to happen between us. What I wanted to happen between us. We were all laughs and googly eyed until we shed our clothes and put our hands on each other. I wanted what Mike had and I got it and it was so damned good. I spent three days with Adeline and thought I was in love. Maybe I was. Maybe I still am. She deserves better than him. When we kissed goodbye, she placed a hand tenderly on my cheek and looked up at me with those soft caramel eyes and said that I helped make her decision, but that she didn't want to see me again.

Now a decade has passed and she still haunts my dreams.

Mike stared at me from across the kitchen table, and I ask him when he had last seen Adeline.

"Before I moved to Italy," he said in barely a whisper.

I scratched Dash on the head and stared at the wall. How long had he been back? Perhaps years. He was stuck in a time warp, pining for a girl he'd lost a decade ago. I didn't want him here, but I couldn't help but feel that I was tied to this moment and maybe the cause of it. I said his name twice but he didn't hear me. I considered reaching across the table for the knife, but it seemed just out of reach. Mike could also see it as an act of mistrust.

"Mike? Mike." He turned toward me with dull eyes. "You have to move on with your life. Do you understand what I'm saying?" He rested an elbow on the tabletop and placed his head in his palm as if the weight were more than he could bear.

"I woke up one day and I couldn't tie my shoes," he said, squeezing the knife. "I wanted to, but I couldn't remember how. And I stared at my shoes. Then I got mad. I wanted to hurt someone, anyone. Her. I spent some time in a place to help me figure things out. A long time. Years I think. They gave me lithium. No one came to see me. Now I'm home and I need to know what's real. Are you real?"

I looked at Dash who responded instantly by pounding his tail against the wall. Mike raised his head and looked at me with dark eyes as if he were trying to read my thoughts.

"Sometimes I'm a ghost watching myself, and I see a stranger and I wonder who he is," Mike said. "Robert, you're the only one I remember who was a true friend. Someone who knows the Mike I was. You're the only person I know. I need a place to stay. I need someone to ground me."

I looked at this man across from me and tried to see the friend I once knew, the friend whose fiancée I screwed, who tutored me in calculus, picked me up when I didn't have gas money, introduced me to girls, worked at my dad's shop when he was flat broke with holes in his shoes and who rose above it all to become successful, only to fall into an abyss that I could never understand. I told Mike that he could stay the night and that I'd even give him some dough, but I'd have to drop him off at his mother's house in the morning. Mike had become an enigma and I didn't trust him. I didn't know what he was capable of.

The house at this moment had a hum all its own. Rain tapped against the windows and patted softly on the roof and I was reminded of something my mother once said. "Nothing like a good hard rain to wash sins into the gutter."

I poured out what remained of my beer and placed that bottle along with the empty vodka in the recycling bin on the back porch. I set Mike up in the spare room, locked my bedroom door and settled in for the night with Dash on the floor snoring. I am a side sleeper but lay on my back staring into the darkness, and I wondered if he knew, if Adeline had told him about me. I wondered if that's why he was here. I thought about what he had said. "Everyone hides in plain sight." Was that meant for me? He asked me if I had a gun in the house. He knew I didn't.

When I heard the creak outside my bedroom door, I placed my hand on the bat, quietly stepped toward the door and imagined myself doing some real damage. Part of me willed that door to open. I wanted Adeline, and I wanted Mike gone.

"What the fuck do you want, Mike?" I said through the door winding up the bat. I sounded breathless, like I'd been running, my wet shirt stuck to my skin. I could practically feel the pressure of his palm on the door. There was no immediate response. I couldn't wait anymore. I unlocked the door, opened it and jumped backed. Mike stood in the hall staring at me dumbfounded. He wavered and placed a hand on the wall for balance. He was shirtless and his big, white belly hung over his tighty-whities.

"Man, shit, Robert, I have to take a leak." Mike slurred his words and looked at me curiously. "Didn't mean to freak you out. I'm all turned around in this old fucking house."

"The other side of the hall," I said. "On the right." I released my grip on the bat feeling foolish and cowardly. I leaned the bat against the wall and scratched Dash on the head and he began swinging his tail wildly. I told Mike I wasn't used to having people in the house. He turned and waved a hand and I watched him shuffle down the hall and enter the bathroom.

I shut the bedroom door and sat on the edge of my bed and Dash nuzzled up to me. He wagged his tail and licked sweat off my face. Light from the bathroom filtered under my bedroom door and I could hear Mike pissing in the guest bathroom. He flushed, shut off the light, walked back to the spare bedroom and shut the door. It was 3:22 in the morning.

My fingers ran over the scar on my right knee and I thought of Adeline, and at that moment, I felt the need to be with her.

Morning sunlight flooded my bedroom and Dash nudged me up a little after seven. The rain and weirdness of the previous night had thrown us off our routine. Mike was snoring when Dash trotted by the spare bedroom. Outside the day had opened-up, the sky was a brilliant blue and the temperature had dropped about 15 degrees. Dash ran around the yard free and crazy in the cool air. I wanted the smell of coffee and quiet in my house. I wanted to feel at home. I made eggs and toast and knocked on Mike's door to rouse him. We ate and he asked if he could stay for another day and I said no and he seemed to sink in his seat.

We drove in silence to his mother's house just a few miles away. As a pretense, we shook hands in the driveway with my new Cherokee idling behind an old Buick LeSabre. The house looked as shitty as it did when we were kids with peeling paint and torn window screens and tall weeds in the yard that depressed me. Mike looked at me with hollow eyes and I saw an emptiness there, but I couldn't help him. I didn't want to help him.

"I've got to go," I said to him.

"I know," Mike said, and stared at me for a long, uncomfortable moment. Then, leaning toward me he said, "The veil has been lifted."

He stood there with his worn leather bag, in his stained suit and watched me drive away. I looked in the rearview before I turned off and he still hadn't moved. He seemed to be staring at the place that I once was, and I felt a great relief.

At the corner, on a lush green lawn, a dozen ibises, as white as cotton, bobbed and pecked at worms beneath the surface. When I drove by, the birds took flight all at once, leaving the worms to their work.

When I walked into my shop later that morning, Dad was there rubbing down one of two mahogany and white maple conference tables with hard wax. He glanced up but didn't say anything. I'd bought the place so he could retire, but that wasn't his style. He always worked a few hours on Sunday morning and I usually stopped by with café con leché and Cuban toast. An old habit.

The air in the shop had the sweetness of cut mahogany. Shafts of sunlight illuminated shining specks of sawdust and it felt good to be there and be a part of something good and honest. I set the coffees down and watched my dad work.

Adeline

Adeline held the girl's hand and whispered to be strong. The girl's glassy eyes stared dully into a void. Her shallow breathing labored through the oxygen mask. The girl moaned and squeezed Adeline's hand in an involuntary spasm and said something, though it sounded more primal and guttural than language.

"Don't talk," Adeline said, watching the girl's vitals on a screen and focusing on her dangerously low blood pressure.

The air had a cool, familiar pungency to it, antiseptic and alcohol mixed with musty body odors, urine, and other bodily fluids.

The girl had entered on a gurney in a mad rush, surrounded by EMTs, trauma nurses, including Adeline, and an ER physician. She now had multiple IVs attached to her arms and wires attached to her chest. Machines surrounding her blinked and sounded off in varying tones, keeping tabs on her tenuous life. As limp as a doll she lay with ghostly translucent skin marred by dried blood and road rash that left crimson blots on the bed sheets.

"Addy, where are we on this one?" the new doctor on duty said, marching in the room. She donned latex gloves and glanced curiously at the colorful silk scarf around Adeline's neck while moving toward the patient.

Adeline rattled off the differential diagnosis in a husky voice that seemed incongruous with her lithe build and soft caramel eyes. "She's finally stable, but barely. Motorcycle wreck. She was the passenger. Deep head lacerations. Stapled in triage." Adeline pointed to the staples and matted blood in the girl's blonde hair. "Skull fracture, chest injuries, abdominal injuries. Blood work came back positive for alcohol and cocaine."

The doctor looked in the girl's blank eyes, called her name and asked if she knew where she was. The girl was unresponsive.

"She's snowed," Adeline said. "EMS gave her eight mils of morphine. Then another four. Said she was combative."

"Assholes," the doctor muttered, moving around the girl. "She's barely over a hundred pounds. I suspect additional fractures. Left humerus. Right scapular. Likely subarachnoid hemorrhaging." The doctor read notes from a computer printout. "We have to get her to the OR, she's losing blood."

"Got it," Adeline said, brushing her thick ponytail behind her and itching the freckles on her nose with the back of her hand. The purple glove on her hand held the strong scent of latex.

"Love your scarf," the doc said to Adeline, punching buttons on the phone. "Brightens things up around here."

"The stethoscope gave me a rash." Adeline touched the scarf self-consciously. "Silk feels better."

Speaking into the phone, the doc asked what surgeon was on duty and said she had a patient for the OR, *stat*, then turned back to Adeline. "I hear you're leaving us."

"I might be staying," Adeline said, and felt her ears get warm and her face flush.

"Oh," the doctor said, stealing a glance at Adeline's hand. Adeline knew she was looking for signs of an engagement ring beneath the latex glove.

"It's for the best," Adeline said, as the doctor moved with purpose toward the next case. Adeline followed the doctor out and turned to see Novia, a tall, black, British RN, glaring from her computer near the adjoining red zone room.

"Might?" Novia whispered angrily, poking the keys at her terminal. "The penny has dropped. Don't be one of those tarts who go back to assholes."

Novia would never understand, and Adeline couldn't explain it.

Mike moved to Newark six months earlier and Adeline had promised to be there in three. Mike didn't have the capacity to be alone and each time Adeline visited, she felt their relationship, and his mental state, deteriorate a little more. They'd been engaged 18 months and she loved him but couldn't commit to his kind of crazy.

Two orderlies showed and they wheeled the girl and the bed out of the ER. Adeline moved along with them, rolling the IV stand and holding the girl's cold hand.

"I'm walking her up," Adeline said to Novia, thinking of the anguished faces she'd seen in the last ten hours; the code blue from a heart attack, a construction worker with two severed fingers, a self-inflicted gunshot wound and the girl who'd been thrown from the motorcycle on I-75. Diarrhea, vomiting, blood, broken bones, suffering, and death all handled with business-like proficiency. Perhaps even dispassionate focus. But the girl, who was about Adeline's age and fighting for her life, reached something inside her. A trauma like that changes a person, Adeline thought. The girl would never be the same. If she lived, she would awake reborn as someone new. Stronger than before.

Adeline arrived from Jersey two days earlier, went straight to Novia's place and they got drunk on Moscow Mules. Adeline wore her new silk scarf, but loosened it with the heat of the alcohol and it fell below the marks on her neck. There was no turning back when Novia's expression changed and she reached for the scarf.

"That fucker should be in jail," Novia said.

"Mike has problems," Adeline said. Even as she said the words, she thought about going back to him. When things were good they were very good. The irony, Adeline thought, was that with all the trauma that Novia saw in the ER, five finger-sized bruises would cause such a stir. Things happen in moments of extreme passion. Love and violence are all too often connected, and ER nurses saw the physical evidence of that almost daily.

Adeline returned from the ICU and saw Novia cooking up mischief with Julie, the charge nurse. Practical jokes were common in the ER. Novia winked at Adeline, and Julie waved her over.

"The girl?" Julie said, to Adeline, shuffling papers at the nurse's station.

"Stable but." Adeline said, and shook her head. "She's in the OR hemorrhaging."

"Two's empty, prep it for the next trauma and help out in the blue zone. Room four is yours," she said without looking up.

Adeline couldn't hide her anger. "What did Novia say to you?" Adeline liked the red zone, the trauma cases. The pressure to make quick decisions for those teetering between life and death, between this world and the next. The space between intrigued her, and that sudden breath of life that brought them back.

"There's a handsome young runner who fell on a sprinkler head and needs a nurse to hold his hand while he gets stitches." Julie smiled.

"Oh bullshit," Adeline said, and looked over at Novia who waved and smiled.

"When a trauma comes, we'll need you," Julie said. "Until then, everybody does their part." She nodded toward room four. "He looks Italian," she whispered.

Adeline prepped room two for the next emergency and took her sweet time about it, then walked across the corridor to the blue zone and played along by shaking ass for the watchful eyes of some amused nurses. She picked up the chart without looking at it and entered room four.

"Adeline," Robert said, flashing his white teeth in a genuine smile. "Nice scarf."

"Robert?" Adeline said, feeling that familiar heat and tingling sensation. She'd only met Robert once and that was with Mike, two years earlier, but there was something there, then and now. She hugged him and he smelled good, even through dried sweat. He was lean and felt like a tendon.

"I thought you were a trauma nurse," Robert said.

"The charge nurse said you were traumatized and needed your hand held," she said, and reached for his hand. Rough. A working man's hand.

Adeline put on latex gloves and examined Robert's leg, below and to the right of the knee. The shin and the calf were streaked with dried blood and wrapped with masking tape. She laughed. "Is this cabinet shop bandaging?"

"Sort of, but I work for a software company now," he said. "I still go in on the weekends to help out. You know, family business."

Adeline heard a gurney roll into the ER along with a hoard of footsteps and the familiar moan of a patient. She hoped she wouldn't get pulled for a trauma.

Robert asked about Mike and said he thought she'd be married and up in Jersey by now.

"That's not going to happen," Adeline said, focusing on removing the tape which was stuck to the hair on his leg. "Fast or slow?" she said, holding the end of the masking tape. He said to go for it. She pulled off the tape quickly, and with it the hair beneath it.

"Thank you, Nurse Ratchet," Robert said and grimaced. "You have such a delicate touch."

"Shut up," she said, watching blood seep from the gash in his leg. Adeline held pressure to it with a gauze. "Have you spoken to him?"

"Not for a long time. I probably won't again," Robert said. "A conversation for another time."

"How'd this happen?" Adeline said, focused on the injury.

"Running. Sidewalk was wet, covered with leaves."

"You need stiches," she said, reaching for his hand to guide it toward the wound. "Hold pressure here and I'll find you a doc. It's going to leave a scar."

Robert held his other hand out and said, "I have so many scars on my hands from the shop I've lost count. They're like permanent memories of painful moments in life. Though I imagine this one," he glanced at his leg, "will always have a bright spot." And he smiled at her.

Adeline looked at Robert and his stupid grin. "A conversation for another time?"

He gestured, and said, "No need to rehash the past."

"You have a cell phone?" she said.

Robert held up his phone. Adeline took it and punched her number on the keypad, let it dial and then hit end. "It's a story I'd like to hear," she said. "Mike's changed."

Robert nodded, as if he knew something about Mike that she didn't. Adeline wanted to know what that was, and she wanted more than that.

"I get off in a few hours," she said. "Will you meet me?"

Robert nodded and seemed genuinely happy about it.

After the doc stitched Robert's leg, Adeline walked back to the red zone smiling. The ER was quiet, and Adeline was nearing the end of her shift. She had the next three days off and a pretty good idea of how she wanted to spend them. Novia asked if she wanted to go out and drink, but Adeline said that she had a date. To which Novia replied, "You dirty little tart."

Before leaving the hospital, Adeline found the girl out of surgery and in the ICU. No one had come to see her. No friends or family. The driver of the motorcycle died at the scene. The girl was placed in an induced coma. She flat-lined in the OR but was revived. The girl now lay in that middle-ground between here and beyond. Adeline sat next to the bed and looked at the girl's arm. The one with the finger-sized bruises. Adeline knew from the yellowing color that they had not occurred in the wreck.

Adeline stared at a bruised banana that hung tenuously on a hook behind the bar, gravity slowing pulling it downward away from its skin.

She turned when Robert arrived and placed a hand on her shoulder. Gently. He gave her a hug and a peck on the cheek. Italians. Hard to get a read on that. Her first time was with a thick, gamey, Italian. She winced. His weight behind her, shoving her face in that desktop with a hand on the back of her head. The stinging sensation. The fullness of it all. And later, sitting in a tub of crimson water, with her mother's voice shouting through the locked bathroom door that it was a school night. The next day in gym class he hardly gave her a glance. But there was something different about Robert, a sweetness. What would he think of her if he knew what had happened to her? If he knew how it had changed her.

Robert ordered a beer to catch up to Adeline who'd been at the bar for an hour. He was neatly dressed in a pair of jeans and white linen shirt and he wore an expensive Swiss watch. He looked damn good, but not in a showy way, not like Mike. Robert seemed comfortable in his own skin.

He looked at the silk scarf around her neck, and though he didn't say anything, Adeline knew it was only a matter of time before she would show him.

"We grew up looking over the fence," Robert said of himself and Mike. "And suddenly he was on the other side looking back, looking down I guess you could say."

Robert liked to talk and gesture with his hands, but Adeline didn't focus on his words. She wanted the feel of his lean body on hers. She wanted his olive skin on hers. Again, it came. The warmth. The tingling. The desire. The ache of emptiness. His eyes were friendly, but distant. Not the look she needed of him.

"What happened to you two?" Adeline said. "You grew up together."

"One night he slipped me acid," Robert said. "Thought it was funny. I didn't trust him after that."

"So, he used drugs?" Adeline said. "Often?" Robert laughed and said that Mike was a mobile pharmacy and used to buy pot from a guy at the cabinet shop.

"He takes some potent anxiety meds and he drinks," Adeline said. "He doesn't want to end up like his father."

"That's odd," Robert said. "His father passed away when we were kids. Heart attack or something."

"He told me his father had a mental breakdown and was institutionalized," Adeline said. "He was embarrassed of that."

They let that lie hang in the air between them, because the truth was a mystery and of no consequence.

Robert said that he was obviously attracted to her, but that he wouldn't fuck Mike over, even if they weren't friends anymore. Even if everything Mike said is a lie.

"We're done," Adeline said, though she wasn't sure she really meant it. Adeline pulled down the scarf revealing the bruises on her neck. Robert cursed and then seemed tongue-tied, even confused. Adeline grabbed his hands and said, "Let's eat some dinner and go back to my place. We'll drink wine and talk some more. This is good medicine for me."

Robert looked at her like a man trying to figure out a puzzle.

Adeline stood and excused herself to the restroom. Two apple martinis on an empty stomach had filled her with bravado. She leaned toward Robert, placed a hand on his inner thigh, kissed him and bit his lower lip. He sat up straight and wide-eyed, like a middle-schooler being flashed by a teacher. He looked at her then, his brain churning behind those eyes. He leaned in and kissed her back, sweetly.

While in the bathroom, Adeline had a sudden thought about the girl and called the ICU. The girl had coded again but was brought back. She was a fighter, that girl. If she came out of it, she'd be someone new. She'd be a survivor.

"Don't move," Adeline said to Robert who stood in her apartment foyer while she proceeded to de-Mike the house as if she were in a footrace. There was no way to rid the place of all the photographs, but a few went into drawers, and a couple she stuffed under the couch. Thank God, the place was clean.

Adeline lived with mysteries. In the ER, patients died of seemingly minor injuries and others hung on despite overwhelming odds, like the girl. Attraction was another mystery. It was chemical, physiological, visual, and visceral, but there was something more. Was Robert forbidden fruit? A chance to fill that emptiness? Was she getting back at Mike? Just maybe it was something real.

"It's nice," Robert said, when she finally walked him around. The place was small, she knew that, a one bedroom, but what more did she need? Adeline handed Robert a bottle of red and said that there was a wine opener in one of the kitchen drawers. "I'm going to freshen up," she said.

He was a man, so Addy didn't need much in the way of advertising, but she didn't want to leave anything to chance. She spritzed perfume, fluffed her hair, took off her bra and put on a thin, white cotton shirt. She imagined herself walking into that kitchen and his eyes taking her in. He'd see right through her shirt and want her.

Addy headed toward the kitchen, ready for his wanting eyes, but when she rounded the corner, Robert wasn't looking. He had one of the kitchen drawers on the countertop and everything emptied out of it. He was working on one of the tracks with a little screwdriver attached to some kind of multitool.

"Robert? What the hell are you doing?" she said.

"The track was loose," Robert said, not glancing back. "The drawer was stuck. I moved one of the screws over. See?" He slid the drawer back into place and turned toward Addy, looking all proud of himself. "Oh," he said, looking at her, dropping his eyes then looking again with conviction. "Ohh."

Worth the wait. His eyes in hers, a slow stroll down her body without shame or self-consciousness and then back up again. She needed that look of desire.

"Leave the drawer. Grab the bottle. There's something I want you to work on in here," Adeline said, and giggled at her own little joke. He followed her, grinning like a kid about to unwrap a mysterious gift.

The first time seemed more like a battle of taking and giving, moving into and against each other. A war of wants. His face on hers. His lean body on her. Exploring hands. Addy put her arms over her head and Robert put his hands in hers and she closed her eyes and enjoyed the feeling of being held captive, pretending that he was leading instead of her. The rhythm was there. Not so fast and wham-bam like Mike. Robert had it right. Slow and driving, but that's not what she needed. It wasn't the fix she desired. Addy couldn't reveal herself. Robert wasn't ready. She held her breath and imagined his hand around her throat. Squeezing. The fight for oxygen. The thrust of power against her. The gush of warmth deep inside. Muscles starving for nourishment. The cusp between here and beyond. Involuntary convulsions of want and ecstasy. Then a deep and sudden inhalation of life, filling her chest, satisfying her body, before collapse.

"Adeline?" She heard the disembodied voice that seemed to be coming from inside her head. "Adeline. What the fuck?" She felt the warmth of Robert's hand on her cheek and opened her eyes, inhaling deeply as the fullness in her receded.

"Robert," she said and smiled. He was still on top of her. "Call me Addy."

"Are you okay?" Robert said. She could just make out his face in the dim light. "I thought you. Did you pass out?"

"I'm wonderful," she smiled and pulled his face toward hers and kissed him with cold lips. "Lay with me," she said, rolling to her side, panting for oxygen.

Addy felt Robert's heartbeat behind her, his chest on her back and a hand cupping one of her breasts. He was warm and gentle and secure, and though he satiated her needs at some level, he would never understand them. Maybe one more day. Just one more day.

"Stay the night," she said.

"I'm not going anywhere," he said, holding her tightly. Then after a moment. "You and Mike are really done?"

"Yes," Addy said in the darkness. Robert held her tightly. She couldn't trust that Mike wouldn't get carried away again with his lust or hurt her during one of his drug induced fits of anger.

Addy said she was surprised that Robert wasn't seeing someone.

"There's a girl at work," Robert said. "Nothing serious. Her father owns the company. They're rich and I'm from the other side of the tracks."

It struck her then, that "looking over the fence" thing that Robert and Mike had in common. They wore those chips like shackles and were bound by their own misguided dreams and expectations of their youth.

"A person can't help how they grew up or who their parents are," Addy said. "Most guys couldn't build a thing if they had a pile of tools in front of them. Own that."

Robert was quiet for a moment.

"You saying I'm good with my hands?" Robert said, with his hands moving gently over her body. She could feel his arousal.

Addy turned over and kissed him, "That's exactly what I'm saying."

Addy awoke in the night with Robert breathing deeply, spooning her. She wanted him to stay the weekend. He'd stay, because he wanted more and she toyed with the idea of Robert in her life. He was the kind of guy that should be in her life. But no matter how she played it out in her mind, it ended badly.

Robert squirmed in his sleep and his watch hit the headboard, making a metallic sound that triggered in Addy, a memory of handcuffs clicking onto the coach's wrists. Adeline recalled vitriol in the voices of the officers echoing in the gymnasium and mingling in the air with the hushed confusion of the other kids in her class. Not once through all his denials did Coach look at her, and Adeline was relieved and so guilty in her delight of the secret she held. For the sake of the other girls he'd violated, he had to go away. Should go away. But he'd unlocked a door to another Adeline, a new Adeline with a self-awareness and a desire that few would understand. The new girl took many years for Addy to fully embrace.

Addy looked into the darkness, held her breath and thought about the girl in the hospital. She believed in her heart that the girl would make it. The girl would open her eyes and take a deep breath of her new life and be born anew with the dawn.

Freeing The Hostages

I walked in the shop, with the air as still as an empty church, to see my dad face down on the concrete floor with a pool of foamy blood having seeped from his mouth, now absorbed by sawdust that accumulated around the saw. That's when the time warp began. I ran to him. Dropped to my knees. Struggled to roll him over. He was thick. Heavy. Not warm. Or maybe I called 911 first. I don't remember. I shouted *Dad*, numerous times. Wiped bloody sawdust from his face and noticed that in one of his hands, he was clutching a wooden folding ruler that once belonged to my great-grandfather.

My dad retired fifteen years ago, but I couldn't stop him from working, so he still came to the shop every day. I grew up working here, and after college, couldn't wait to start a career someplace else. Eventually, I came back and bought the place. Everyone who worked here left at some point, but they always came back. Today, Dad came back after dinner to borrow some tools for a home project. My mother called when she couldn't get a hold of him. His phone went to voicemail and I knew there was no way he was behind the saw this late at night. I had a sickly feeling in my gut on the drive back to Ybor City.

Doing chest compressions winded me and I blurted words in short bursts to the woman on the phone with the calming voice. I continued pumping my dad's barrel chest to the refrain from the Bee Gees song, "Stayin' Alive." I'd been married a few years and my wife, my second wife, was a trauma nurse in an emergency room. She once told me that song was a good way to keep the rhythm when doing chest compressions. I never thought the occasion to use that knowledge would arise.

Droplets of sweat from my face made dark stains on Dad's light blue, button-down. He gurgled and a foamy liquid oozed from his mouth. My arms burned and I was winded, but I didn't stop. I couldn't stop. EMTs appeared behind me and prodded me to move. They asked me questions. I don't remember what they asked or what I told them. One of them immediately went to work pumping his chest, as I had, while the other ran out to bring in equipment. I backed up until I hit one of our low work tables and sat on the rough surface, speckled with dried glue and paint. My wet clothes stuck to my body and felt like an additional layer of skin.

I closed my eyes and filled my lungs with the scent of ash and maple, and it was comforting, the smell of wood in the air. The smell I grew up with that reminded me of my dad, though when I was a kid it was mostly pine. He carried it with him always, the scent of wood, even after he showered and was clean. And I carried it with me. I looked around the shop and each corner held a victory that I could picture. The way he nodded and narrowed his eyes after I built my first dovetail drawer. Learning how to read a set of plans and then planning cuts to get the most out of a sheet of wood. Changing out saw blades and knowing when the blade was dull. He taught me how to replace the bushings in the big sander, set up a dado blade on the table saw and square a cabinet. Huge victories for a boy.

I remember the look in his eyes the day I quit, like a light had suddenly burned out, and how he swelled with pride when I came back five years later.

Looking up, I noticed that the skylight window was open, and through the window, the stars and a crescent moon lay against a deep purple sky. Then, something else caught my eye. Something I had not noticed before. A wispy movement. Barely visible. Probably impossible to see in the daylight. Strands of rope, just a few inches long, caught on the sharp edge of the window, oscillating with the night breeze. And I thought, what are the chances, after more than thirty years? To see tangible evidence of the moment I first lost part of my father.

"Roberto, you okay?" my father called through that open skylight window high above my head.

"The ladder fell," I shouted. "The rope hurts." Tears streamed down my cheeks as I dangled in the darkness.

My fall from the ladder was stopped short by the rope under my arms and around my chest, which cut into my sides, burned my skin and forced an anguished, involuntary sound from my scrawny ten-year-old body. The violent jolt squeezed water from my eyes and air from my lungs. The aluminum ladder, which slid off the wall, hit the concrete floor and sounded like an explosion. I placed my sneakers and hands against the cool cement wall that stopped me from swinging and thought I could hear rats scurrying under my feet, though I couldn't see them in the dark. The rope creaked as I reached for the flashlight in my back pocket. It must have fallen out. The place smelled familiar with the scent of wood hanging in the air, but in the black it was all a mystery.

"We're going to lower you to the floor," Dad said. "Nothing is going to hurt you in there. It's the same shop you see in the daylight."

Far above my head through the small rectangular window, I could see the stars and a crescent moon against a deep purple sky. My father's voice and presence were just beyond the concrete wall, yet I was alone in the dark, and hurting.

"Don't let the rats eat you," my brother said.

"*Stunod*," my father shouted at my brother.

I could hear the other adults outside laugh; Mr. Pernell, a big, bearded man who never said very much, and Sarge, a retired Marine. Both worked at the shop.

The ride to the floor was jerky because the rope kept getting caught on the metal edge of the open window, and with each drop, it cut into my skin and squeezed my chest. It hurt, but I didn't want to get made fun of by the men, or by my brother. I was integral to this mission. My dad said so. We were there to free the hostages from Garibaldi.

The EMTs worked vigorously, while my dad's limp body shook. Their physical movements held the air of desperation. One of them gave Dad a shot, while the other cut his shirt open. They rubbed something over his barrel chest, one of them shouted, "clear" and put the paddles on him. His body stiffened violently, and it was painful to watch.

I knew at some point, I'd have to call my mother. I thought back to that night and the argument that preceded our midnight run to free the hostages.

"Johnny. It's the middle of the night. These boys don't need to be involved in this." My mother stood in the hallway wearing the pink robe and slippers we'd gotten her for Mother's Day. Dad sat at my bedside with his thick, leathery hand on my cheek coaxing me up.

My mother cursed in Italian and threw her hands up.

In the van, Sal took the passenger seat like he always did, and I sat between the two seats on a packing blanket that my dad threw over the toolbox. The roads were quiet, and no one said a word on the drive to Ybor City. I remember continually yawning out of exhaustion and nervousness, wondering what my role would be and why we had to go in the middle of the night. When we arrived, my dad didn't enter our parking lot, but instead, pulled through the alley and parked the van and our trailer in the grassy area behind the shop. Mr. Pernell and Sarge were waiting for us there with a thick brown rope and an aluminum extension ladder they'd leaned against the outside of the building. It led to a small, second story window that opened outward at the bottom, like a wedge.

Looking up, I froze and said, "Why me?"

"Your brother will never fit through that window," Dad said.

My brother, Sal, took after my dad's side of the family. He was fourteen, built like a block and weighed 120 pounds. He played football and wrestled and all the men in the family gave him a lot of attention. There was no way he could squeeze through that window, much less get lowered with a rope. I took after my mother's side. I was ten and weighed about 50 pounds, so I won the job of saving the shop from ruin.

I trembled as the men secured the rope around my chest. Dad stuffed the flashlight in my back pocket and followed me up the ladder saying not to look down.

Bright yellow tape with the red letters, IRS, sealed the doors to the shop. Dad said that if we broke the seals, Garibaldi would know and we'd get in trouble. "Our cabinets are being held hostage," he said.

The garage doors locked from the inside, so Garibaldi did nothing to secure them. That was his mistake. Before Dad and his workers were ordered out of the shop, he made sure to unlock one of the skylight windows and leave an aluminum extension ladder leaning against the inside wall, as if it belonged there. The ladder was left for me.

"This is how we do it in Ybor City," my dad said, at one point in the night.

The EMTs exchanged a look and something was communicated between them. It was an exchange they'd shared before. After that, one of them cocked his head back at me and the story was written in his eyes and it felt like the clenching of a fist in my chest. A feeling washed over me with the sweat that covered my body. I'd never felt more alone or more alive with pain. Like that scared little boy, hanging from a rope in a darkened shop.

When my feet hit the floor, I said so and my father said to wriggle out of the rope. "Don't turn on the lights," he said. "Just unlock the garage door."

"I can't see anything," I shouted. "I lost the flashlight." I used my T-shirt to wipe sweat from my forehead and water from my eyes. In that moment, I felt something that was once part of me, was gone leaving a hole inside me that filled with a sudden and painful knowledge.

"You know the shop." Dad's voice sounded faint now. He must have climbed down the ladder. "Walk along the concrete wall. We cleared a path for you."

I did as I was told quickly, pretending I wasn't afraid, then felt a wave of relief when they pulled up the garage door and I saw my father, brother, Mr. Pernell and Sarge standing in the alley with flashlights. My father gave me a hug and said he was proud of me, but not to tell anyone. Ever. "And don't tell your mother," he said. "Women don't understand these things."

I didn't question this, but it made me feel weird and powerful.

Dad told me to sit in the cab of the van while they loaded the cabinets onto the trailer. I was hesitant about sitting outside alone in the dark. Sarge rubbed my head and handed me his flashlight while my dad, my brother and Mr. Pernell went into the shop.

"Robert, why don't you open the van doors, stand in the back and point that flashlight into the trailer," Sarge said. "That will help us when we load the cabinets." I liked that idea. It kept me closer to the garage door.

"Sarge," I said, before he went in the shop, "are we breaking the law?"

Sarge was a big black man with a gentle way about him. He had friendly eyes and a deep voice, like he could sing bass in one of those barbershop quartets. He crossed his arms and pondered my question for a moment and said, "I'll tell you. Your daddy, he's a good man with a big heart. He knows that sometimes the right thing to do isn't always the best thing to do."

I screwed my face up at this wonderfully twisted logic.

"Check it out my man," Sarge said. "We built these cabinets. We're going to deliver them to the people who ordered them and get paid. They deserve their cabinets. Right? With that money, your daddy is going to pay the IRS."

"You mean, Garibaldi?" I said.

Sarge laughed. "Yeah, Garibaldi. The shop's going to get reopened, we're all going to go back to work and Mr. Pernell and I, and your daddy can make a living, put food on the table, pay our bills, put our kids through college. Everybody gets what they want and it don't hurt nobody. It's the best thing."

"But not the right thing?" I said.

Sarge gestured with his hands and said to point the flashlight into the trailer. He went into the shop to help with the loading.

It seemed like I held that flashlight for hours. They filled up our trailer and tied down the cabinets. Then we filled a trailer attached to Sarge's truck. As I watched and pointed the flashlight where the men needed it, I realized that my fear had faded. Nothing could hurt me. It was one-thirty in the morning when we pulled out of the alley and I could see a smile on my dad's face.

"We did it, didn't we, Dad?" I said.

He nodded. "I'm proud of you boys. Tonight, you were men. You did men's work. Let's go to Village Inn for pancakes."

It was the best night of my life.

When I awoke the next morning, Dad had gone. He went to deliver the cabinets we'd liberated. My brother snored in the other twin bed. His clothes and mine were splayed out on the floor between our beds. I sat up shirtless and in pain from the rope burns across my chest and under my arms. It felt like I was on fire. When I heard my mother in the hall, I lay back down, pulled the covers to my neck, and feigned sleep. The door squeaked and I knew she was there. When the door quietly shut, I opened my eyes, went to my dresser and put on a T-shirt. I couldn't let her see the burns. It wasn't the right thing, but I knew it was the best thing.

The EMTs both looked at me now with defeat in their eyes.

"It's okay," I said to the them. "It's okay. All he's known is work. It's time for him to rest. That's how we do it in Ybor City." And they seemed relieved.

I looked at my dad's hand and asked one of the EMTs to hand me the wooden ruler. He nodded, gently slid the ruler from my father's grasp, and gave it to me. I squeezed that ancient ruler in my hands.

JOSEPH ALLEN COSTA

Notes and Acknowledgements

Thank you to the many readers, editors, and mentors who helped to shape this collection. First and foremost, my incredible wife (and first reader) Teresa, who encouraged me to pursue an MFA in creative writing, and whose tough love and critical eye saved many of these stories from mediocrity.

My deepest thanks to the wonderfully talented writers and mentors at the University of Tampa Low Residency MFA program, including Brock Clarke, Jason Ockert, Kevin Moffett, and program director Erica Dawson.

Thank you to S.R. Stewart, Kristen Marckmann, Chandler White and the amazing team at Unsolicited Press for publishing this collection and sharing in my vision.

Finally, thank you Dad, for everything. Without you, this book would not have been possible, and the smell of sawdust wouldn't put a smile on my face, as it always does.

A sincere thank you to the literary magazines and journals that published stories from this collection. These include:

"Comets" and "Fly Away Home" BULL
"Involuntary Memory" The Write Launch
"Undercurrent" Rabble Lit
"The Hygienist" HCE Review
"Sinners and Saints" December magazine Vol. 30.1.

JOSEPH ALLEN COSTA

Afterward

The first cabinet shop, a white wooden structure built in the early nineteen hundreds, stood on 19th Avenue in Ybor City (Tampa's Latin Quarter) directly next to the sagging, white cassata — otherwise known as a bungalow — where my father was born. There, in the nineteen thirties and forties, his father ran Costa, Barber and Beauty Equipment, delivering, tonics, ointments, chairs, combs, brushes, razors, scissors and other accoutrements of the industry throughout Central Florida. By the early nineteen fifties, after a stint in the Marine Corps, my dad took over and began building cabinets. The name, Costa, Barber and Beauty Equipment, remained for a while, but eventually changed to Shoreline Specialties as the business and product lines changed. Though my dad continued to build cabinets for barbershops and salons, he designed and built more custom kitchens, desks and office equipment.

I do recall as a boy of eight or nine, being handed a rag and bottle of mineral spirits to clean glue off cabinets, or given a broom and told to sweep sawdust, or wind extension cords or put tools away. That was Dad's daycare. If he gave me something to do, he'd always know where I was. Mom worked full-time as the bookkeeper for a chain of clothing stores, so my two older brothers and I worked with Dad, most weekends and virtually every day over the brutal Florida summers. Occasionally, my younger sister worked in the office filing, or drove around picking up materials.

Each year, we'd take off one week during summer to spend at Indian Rocks Beach, forty-five minutes west of Tampa. Dad would spend a couple of days at the beach, then head back to the shop. Eventually, he sold that property and moved the shop to the south side of Ybor City, near the banana docks. During my first year of college, Dad bought a small building north of downtown Tampa, and by the early eighties, had about ten people working for him. They were a tossed salad of ethnicities, nationalities, races and ages. The shop had two shifts, a day shift and night shift. Dad worked both. That's the shop I remember most.

My dad had the shop in five locations over sixty years. The shop depicted in *Comets* is an amalgamation of all those shops, thus, the shop in these stories is both real and fictional. But anyone who worked at the shop and knew my dad, in reading this collection, will recognize the place and the spirit imbued by the stories. Like Johnny Lazzara, the dad depicted in *Comets*, the shop was my father's church and working sixty, or seventy-hour weeks was not out of the ordinary. The real Johnny, my dad, worked this way until he was eighty. In reading the stories collected here, those who knew my father will recognize much of his true character in my fictional character, but there will be much they don't recognize as well, the fictional side.

Like Robert, the throughline protagonist, I learned to hate the shop before I learned to love it, then to miss it. Other than that, Robert and I have little in common. But how lucky was I, to get an opportunity to work with my dad for more than a dozen years and learn a trade. I cherish those days and all of the hard-working men from whom I learned so much.

People don't train to be cabinetmakers. There are no trade schools for the craft. You're either born into it, or you learn the trade doing the work. The men who worked for my dad fell into cabinetmaking and into the shop by happenstance. Some were guys who lived their lives teetering on financial disaster, while others were artisans who made it their life's endeavor and found happiness in that. They were all looking for something different, but found common ground in that shop, seeking a means of survival, a few extra dollars in their pockets and the satisfaction that comes with building something of quality with your hands. They were all comets on varying cyclical journeys, each coming and going, quitting and returning, all revolving around the old man, the rock, a force of gravity, always greeting them back with open arms for as long as they wanted to work.